Novel Slices

Issue Five

Cover Artwork
by Alya

Subscriptions for two issues annually are:

$20/year, digital format (pdf or epub) or

$30/year for print issues

See our website for more info:

www.novelslices.com/issues

Twice annually, Novel Slices publishes the five winners of our novel excerpt contest. Entries can be made in March/April and September/October each year through our website at www.novelslices.com/contest

Contest Judge   Santiago R. Vaquera-Vásquez
Founding Editor   Hardy Griffin
Editor   Stephanie Johnson

All five excerpts in this issue are equal first-place winners in the Novel Slices contest. The editors have chosen the order here solely for the flow of subjects and styles.

Table of Contents

Editor's Note

We knew it was coming and now it's here: All of the winning excerpts in this issue are brilliant examples of genre fiction!

In reverse order, Sean Connell's *A Forever Opposition* begins as a tale of a husband's revenge for his wife's overdose but then—well, I simply can't ruin the surprise. And Shawn Goodman's *The Satin Gunmetal Sky* is sure to become a new classic in the vein of *Blade Runner*, delving into the worst side of humanity and why a 'synth' simply might refuse to pass as human.

Katie Tomasko's *Sorry, Maggie May* is that rarest of gems, a ghost story that isn't a horror but looks instead at what it means when we can't let someone go. Then, in Louise Kantro's *Seconds* we find ourselves with three brave children imprisoned in the liminal space of the foster-care system but who find the most unlikely of saviors—it feels like the best Middle Grade and Young Adult writing where it's really for avid readers of all ages. The introductory excerpt in this issue is in some ways indefinable—at turns it seems a psychological thriller, á la *Girl on a Train*, at others it's a medical mystery like *Memento*.

We want to thank our esteemed judge, Santiago R. Vaquera-Vásquez for what is admittedly not an easy job! The cover art spoke to us about the new heights of the *Novel Slices* community: We are overjoyed to announce that our next judge, Damyanti Biswas, is the author of *The Blue Bar*, and was a winner of the second *Novel Slices* contest. So we've come full circle! Last but far from least, if you will be at the AWP conference in March, come by booth 220 and see us—we'll be raffling great prizes all three days!

—Hardy

The Listener

Celeste White

Chapter One: Christopher

What I remember: How to get dressed. How to make toast. How to walk, sit, lie, and stand. How to speak. What a skillet is for, what a toothbrush is for, what a mailbox is for. How to raise and lower my blinds.

What I don't remember: My name. Where I live. How I got here. What I do for a living. Any of my neighbors, or whether I have family.

My surroundings and furnishings seem oddly familiar, but in a vague sort of way, as if I had dreamed about them and now the dream is fading. The dresser in the corner of my bedroom sits placidly in the early morning sun, its scuffed pecan skin promising an elusive intimacy; the chrome and clay-colored linoleum kitchen table appears to offer nothing but an echo of shared lunches and dinners. I infer that I live alone because no one else has made an appearance inside my home, and I can find no clothing other than that which seems to belong to me: no lingerie, dresses, nor feminine shoes. No miniature clothes for a child. All the clothes that I have found in my closet and drawers—the soft, worn jeans and gabardine slacks, the comfortable T shirts and casual button-down shirts—fit me.

I awakened a few days ago with no recollection of what had happened the day before. Or the day before that, or the day before that. I lay in bed for an hour, hoping that memories would start to surface. But none did. I had the presence of mind to surmise that I might have suffered a small stroke or a seizure, and I knew to look up a doctor in the phone book. I knew how to dial the number and make an appointment. But despite various tests and a thorough physical examination, nothing wrong could be found—no paralyzed limbs nor droopy facial features plagued me; no brain tumor nor aneurism showed itself in the scans performed.

"It could be a case of transient global amnesia," the doctor told me, a heavy-set, middle-aged man with a resemblance to a snub-faced dog that I encountered on my walk to his office. No automobile was parked in my garage, and I could find no keys for a car anywhere in my house. Fortunately, the town that I live in—Clear Springs, the phone book had informed me—is small.

"It could have been brought on by any number of things," he speculated; "immersion in cold water, a bump on the head, acute emotional distress, or..." he added, with a coy wink at odds with his jowly, ponderous features, "sexual intercourse."

I strained to think—had any of these things happened to me the day before? I hadn't found any wet clothes in my bathroom nor laundry, and a cautious probe of my head didn't reveal any lumps or sore places. As for intercourse— well, that was the most auspicious possibility, but so far, no one has called to tell me what a sublime experience we had and to inquire when we might get together again.

He told me that global transient amnesia—or GTA, for short—usually resolved itself within twenty-four hours. "So if your memory doesn't return after the weekend, give me a call," he said. He handed me his card, which I stuffed in my pocket.

It is now Monday and my memory has not returned, but I find myself unwilling to call him. I'm not sure why. Perhaps because I didn't get the impression that he had many tricks left up his sleeve, and I don't care for the idea of additional tests and examinations. In the meantime, this is what I have found:

I have no cell phone, which I am learning almost everyone possesses. There is not one scrap of paper in my home to give me a clue as to my identity. No bills, no credit cards, no tax returns, no memberships in clubs, frequent buyer programs, nor even secret societies. I discovered a nice bit of cash in my wallet (which contained none of the above-mentioned items, including a driver's license), which is how I paid the good doctor. And I did come across a few photographs of both sandy and rocky beaches; yet they possess no identifying information on the backs, and nothing about the scenery indicates where the pictures might have been taken.

I hoped that someone might pay me a visit or call, but so far, no one has. I appear to have no address book nor anything at all along those lines, so there is no one familiar for me to contact.

The most remarkable find? A closet off the living room that contains an extraordinary bureau, one hidden underneath a canvas tarp, an array of jackets, and a plaid wool blanket whose size indicates it might serve well for picnics or outdoor theater events. The bureau looks to be made of a smooth red cherry, darkened by the years. The simple round knobs appear to be carved from the same wood. No ornament decorated it that I could see—when I first laid eyes on it. But as I continued to gaze at it, an exquisite silver filigree became visible along the rails and the face. And then

4

the knobs began to glow as if lighted from their interiors, turning first crimson, then amber.

When I overcame my astonishment, I carefully opened the drawers and found them all to be empty, except one. And in that drawer, I found a thousand dollars. I assumed that this must be my rainy day fund, but the amount of money seemed too much to stash in such a cavalier manner. I thought of depositing it in a bank, but then it occurred to me that, not only had I not found a bank book nor check book, I still hadn't found anything that had my name on it.

The doctor had filed my medical information under the name, "John Doe," telling me that I could call him when my memory returned and he would have his staff update my records. Despite the fact that this has not happened yet, I'm not content to be a John Doe. The blandness of the name carries a strange menace, eliciting associations with murder victims, so I decided to invent a name for the time being. And when—I hope for "when," not "if"—I remember my identity, I can substitute my real name. I decided to call myself Christopher Seabright, feeling a strong yearning in my heart whenever I look at the photos I have of beaches. And for some reason I can't explain, I have the impression that I might have been a sailor at one time. But if that were so, where is my boat? And why am I living inland?

When all the searches of my home produced nothing more of note, I thought to call upon my neighbors, see if any of them could tell me my real name and enlighten me as to my occupation and circumstances. But then it occurred to me that I might be hiding. From what or whom, I have no idea. But my house is so devoid of any clues as to my identity that it seems suspicious, deliberate. It even occurred to me that this isn't my home—that I had ensconced myself here when I found no resident and I was on the run from... what?

For a few blinding, panicked moments, I even wondered if I had dispatched the previous resident. But if that were the case, would the clothes here fit me so well? I suppose they could. They could.

But I have found no signs of a struggle, and no policemen have shown up to check on anyone's disappearance, nor to ask me what I am doing here instead of the rightful resident. And if no one is calling me, no one is calling anyone else here, either.

What to do? How to proceed? I simply am not content to haunt the rooms of this house and hope for memories to return; that doesn't come naturally. Some kind of action seems called for.

As I sit on the sofa in my den, my eyes fall once more upon the phone book that I used to find my doctor. I pick it up, wondering if I might find my address listed, and with it, my name. As I riffle through the thin pages, however, I realize what a gargantuan task that could be, even for a town the size of Clear Springs. Then an entry leaps out at me: Beaulieu, Violet: Listener. The concept seems somewhat peculiar—what, exactly, does a Listener do? And of course, I have nothing to tell her, except my impoverished mystery of not knowing who I am.

Even so. I hold my breath and dial her number. I make an appointment for two days hence. Her voice is lovely, reminding me of melted honey and warm, slanted afternoon light. Perhaps a Listener can hear more than the human voice or story tells. Perhaps a Listener can hear echoes, lost memories, hidden secrets. Perhaps a Listener can hear things both untold and forgotten. I can hope, anyway. Because hope is one of the few things I have to hold onto. I feel as though I'm drowning, and hope is the shining life preserver bobbing in the waves.

Chapter Two: Violet

I listen; that's what I do. But it's not as easy as you might think.

Not that I don't love the stories. I love the stories. And there are more amazing ones than you can imagine, from people whose lives, from the outside, appear utterly mundane and bland. As a matter of fact, just this morning a man wandered into my office with "nondescript" stamped all over him, wearing a pale blue, short-sleeved Oxford shirt, a brown tie hanging from his neck like a flattened salami, and shiny polyester pants just a shade too short, revealing thin, piped brown socks above his loafers. The latter were heartrendingly adorned with leather tassels whose tips had curled up into unintended joviality. His face resembled a baby's face—soft and unformed, round and dewy—except for the boxy, black-rimmed glasses that gave him the appearance of the bookkeeper he was.

I often like to imagine the person's story before he begins. When I first undertook this work, of course, I thought I should keep my mind as empty and blank as a freshly washed, white contour sheet fitted over the mattress before anything else has been added. That way, I would have no preconceptions. My client's story and hers alone would then fill my consciousness with its juicy, succulent uniqueness, its surprising twists and turns, its unexpected rhythms and beats. But in practice, I found that this rarely works. No, it's impossible not to have preconceptions; it's better to indulge in my preconceptions, to lay them out before me frankly and unapologetically. Because quite honestly, it's much more fun to be wrong than to be right.

So this morning I was thinking when I first laid eyes on

this man: He's having an affair. He's having a torrid, passionate affair with a young woman half his age. She shaves her head in order to reveal an elaborate tattoo of a Celtic cross and she wears a stud through her tongue in order to give her lover the most rapturous oral sex he's ever had. She attends Burning Man Festivals and follows her favorite jam band all over the country. Occasionally, he joins her and they make love in cheap motels. Sometimes they dine on the scraps of fast food that previous guests have left stashed in the drawer of the bedside table and that the perfunctory housekeeping has overlooked, just to be perversely disgusting and to take a ridiculous risk that has no pay-off whatsoever, simply for the thrill of taking chances. He loves his wife, he really does, but he's unable to resist the sexual charge of this forbidden union, something he never, ever thought would happen to him, certainly not at his age.

But I revealed nothing of this. As I said, I listen. Instead, I said to him, "Mr. Culpepper, please have a seat." I gestured to the deep, comfy armchair that faced mine across my desk. "What have you come to tell me about today?"

He sank into the chair, avoiding eye contact. This is often the case and it doesn't bother me. What matters is that they speak up, if I'm to do my job. He cleared his throat. "Well," he said, "it's a rather unusual situation."

"I understand," I said, nodding encouragingly.

He pursed his lips, placed both hands on the arms of the chair, looking up, now, at the ceiling. "In fact, Miss Beaulieu, I'm not sure how to begin."

"What I find," I said, "is that it's often best to begin in the middle. That way, you don't get bogged down in the beginning."

"Oh," he replied, a little startled. "Well, that makes sense."

I gave him a smile and waited. This is not the difficult part. I've honed my patience throughout the years, as I've learned that prompting someone to tell his story is never a good idea. A good story needs to tumble out of its own accord, impelled by its need to be released.

"The other day," he finally murmured, giving me an apologetic smile, "I went to an art show."

"Splendid," I said—one of my favorite words. Granted, it's a little out of date, but really, it's an outstanding word. Try it out. You'll see. The "spl" sound coupled with the satisfyingly nasal "n" gives the palate a lovely mini-workout, and the stuttery little "did" tacked onto the end is nothing short of sheer delight to enunciate.

"Yes, well, it's not something I ordinarily do. I work long hours at my company, and I'm married and I have a family. When I'm not at work, I'm usually at home, spending time with my family."

I nodded.

"But for some reason, one day, on my lunch hour, I was walking past this art guild that's near my office, and I felt compelled to go in."

"These things happen," I said.

"Well, not to me, they don't."

"I see." I didn't know it yet, but Mr. Culpepper was about to reveal a secret far more exciting and grand than the passion I had imagined for him.

"I have no idea why I went in there. None. But when I did, I spotted this painting. It was small. Nothing showy. Nothing fancy. It was a quiet painting, I would say."

"Mm-hm."

"It was only about twelve inches square. It was a landscape. A country scene. A brilliant green field with a tiny little house way in the distance. The sky was dark, overcast.

Gray. But in the window of the house there was this glistening yellow light that, well—pierced me." He stopped, fumbled in his breast pocket for a handkerchief. Once he had it in hand, he removed his glasses and dabbed at his eyes. "It pierced me to my very soul," he added, his voice swollen with emotion. His eyes, without the glasses, looked entirely different: the startling, incandescent blue of a gap in the clouds.

"It sounds," I said, "like a transcendent experience."

"Well, it was," he replied defensively. He sighed, wiped his face, now, with the handkerchief. "The problem is, this—this feeling doesn't fit anywhere else in my life. I bought the painting, but that wasn't enough. I crave beauty now when I never needed it before. My wife, God bless her, is not a beautiful woman, but that's not the problem. I love my wife. She's a good woman. The problem is that she can't see beauty. I never minded that before, never did. But now I do. I want my home to be beautiful, I want my yard to be beautiful. I—" here his voice broke— "I want to be beautiful." He dabbed once more at his eyes, laughing with embarrassment and self-derision. "And how ridiculous is that? I'm plain. I'm lumpy. I was never handsome even as a boy. And now that I'm middle-aged, well—" He stopped, replaced his eye glasses, looking down at the floor.

This is where listening gets hard. People bare their souls. They share their agony, their pain. You want to give them advice, you want to give them some pithy insight. But I've learned that if people don't reach insights on their own, if they don't come up with their own good advice, it doesn't do any good to tell them. It won't stick. It will fade away like a dream, only half-remembered. What could I tell him? That his desire for beauty was beautiful in and of itself? That when he was telling me about this painting, touched to the

10

point of tears and so winsomely vulnerable, he was beautiful in that moment?

Or that he could, perhaps, start with his tie?

Instead, I said, "It's true you're middle-aged. But that's a neutral fact, no different from saying your name is Mr. Culpepper. It's a starting point. Everything is a starting point, in fact." I paused. "If there was one thing you could change in your life right now, what would it be?"

"Why, I don't really know."

"Just one little thing. It could be anything."

"Well, I suppose I would like to change the curtains in the living room. I've never liked them. The color's oppressive, sort of the color of a tadpole, and they have an abstract pattern on them that reminds me of fried eggs. I've never liked fried eggs."

"Uh-huh."

"And if the pattern's supposed to be abstract, I don't want it to remind me of anything. You know? It's annoying."

"Sure," I said. "Once you changed the curtains, is there something else you might like to do?"

He pondered, bringing his fingertips together and touching his plump, soft lips. "Well, I think I'd like to have cut flowers in the house. That could get expensive, of course. But if I planted more flowers in my yard, I could have them just for the taking."

"Yes, you could."

"And once I did that," he continued, excitement beginning to creep into his voice, "why, I could—I could start drying them. And making wreaths!"

"Wreaths are a lovely idea," I said.

"I could take my wife shopping," he said dreamily. "Encourage her to get clothes she never thought she was pretty enough to wear."

11

"It's amazing," I said, "how people can transform."

He sat with a small, dreamy smile on his face for a few moments, then startled me by yelping, "Yes!" and throwing his hands into the air. He let them drop, began to fiddle absentmindedly with his tie. His neckwear caught his eye then and he frowned. "I could throw away this tie!" he exclaimed. "I've always hated this tie! It looks like a turd, for God's sake. My boss gave it to me and I always thought I had to wear it to please him. But no more, damn it! Damn this stupid tie!" In a furious, scrabbling motion, he clawed the tie from his neck, wadded it up, threw it down on the floor. "There!" he said. He stood up and stomped on it. "Stupid, stupid turd of a tie!"

This set me to giggling, which at first earned me an annoyed and astonished glare from Mr. Culpepper. But before long, we were both giggling our heads off, gasping for breath. And I'm telling you, by the time Mr. Culpepper left my office, he was glowing. He was beautiful. Oh, was he! The human spirit is a sublime entity, it really is. The human spirit is anything but nondescript. And people's secret lives—no matter how encrusted over by shopping addictions or reality TV fixations or cleaning fetishes they might be in the world outside of my beloved Clear Springs—are, generally speaking, amazingly rich. Sweetly, gorgeously, drippingly rich.

Almost always, however, people's stories can be told in one session. Just one session. And I've always liked that closure. I usually never see these people again, except when our paths cross in the community, where, having revealed their secret lives, to me and to themselves, they now carry about them a new majesty.

I suppose that I might be the only person alive who doesn't have a secret life. I've never felt the need for one.

But lately, I've been wondering if I'm missing out on something. The problem is, you can't just decide to have a secret life. A secret life, it seems to me, is one that grows out of forbidden longing, hopeless yearning, frustration, or guilt. I have never felt these things. It's simple, my life. I've always had everyone else's stories to enrich my days. Still, I wonder. Have I, by listening so much and having so little of my own to tell, become two-dimensional?

Well, it's a valid question, but at the same time, I don't really know what to do about it. Go out and create some high drama just so I will have a story, too? So I could tell it to… whom? Myself? It doesn't seem practical. And if I'm two-dimensional, doesn't that make me a better listener? A figurative sounding board—this is what I should aspire to, if I'm to be good at my job. Plenty of people with stories exist out there. Doesn't there also need to be an audience, those of us who listen, receive… absorb? And honestly, what could be better than coming in to work day after day listening to stories? It's like getting paid to nap or eat chocolate.

And yet. I can't explain it, but something has been gnawing at the edges of my consciousness lately, nibbling away at my sense of ease. I haven't put my finger on the problem yet, but I do get the strong impression that leaving it alone might court disaster. A rather hyperbolic impression, to be sure. But one that I can't shake. I open my appointment book and scan the contents, wondering if anything there might offer any clues.

Nothing jumps out. But I remember now a phone call from yesterday, from a gentleman calling to make an appointment. There was something about his voice… something haunted and haunting, but enchanting, too—a voice as bleak as a winter's night yet as promising as a surprise package arriving in the morning mail. Perhaps this stranger—for I recognize neither his voice nor his name—might provide me with a clue.

I can't decide: Do I find the thought tantalizing or terrifying?

Chapter Three: Christopher

I dreamed last night. Or, more accurately perhaps, I remembered my dreams: I am sitting on the sand in warm climes. The sun cradles me with kindly beams while the wind scoots past me, soft and skirling. I am viewing the action from "my" eyes, the eyes of a child, I surmise, because the hands that are happily patting the sides of a sand castle are small and chubby, the wrist bones tender dimples. I am filled with pure joy and contentment, of a degree I can barely comprehend, when I look up to see another small figure being swallowed up by the waves. I can see the head only—a cap of bright curls that glints in the sunlight, gold to the silver of the spindrift as it froths into the sky. But soon, even that disappears, to my deep and utter confusion. I awakened then, gasping and shaking, full of despair. Worse—it was not even close to dawn. My bedside clock informed me that it was three o'clock.

I considered rising anyway, but the yawning emptiness of my current predicament discouraged me. I turned to my other side and clutched the blanket for comfort, poor though it might be. And when I fell asleep once more, I dreamed of sailing on inky waters under a flat, baleful moon, my ship dwarfed by the mountainous waters... waters that morphed into hillocks of frozen snow... or was it ash?... ash that glittered in the watchful moonlight like shards of glass, speckling the sere landscape that drew me ever deeper into darkness. I dreamed that I awakened several times, only to realize that I was still dreaming, of the night and the pale, floating moon, of water so massive and deep it pinned my body to the belly of the rocking ship, of air so icy sharp it sliced the soft tissue in my lungs. When I finally did awaken in the morning, I felt as if I had swum through the ether to the farthest extremities of the universe and back again.

Not the most auspicious beginning to my day.

My appointment with the Listener is not until tomorrow, and I don't understand the impatience I feel in wanting to see her. I have no reason to believe that she might be able to help me; perhaps I am grasping at straws. Yet, what else do I have to grasp? This morning, I've decided, I will visit one or two of my neighbors. I can't imagine an endless existence where I lurk inside my home with no knowledge of what has brought me—or imprisoned me— here. If I am to expose myself to harm or danger, better now than never. Nothing happened to me on my way to or from the doctor's office. I will have to leave this house to keep my appointment with Violet Beaulieu. Courage and action appeal to me much more than passivity and fear. If I am to encounter a nefarious destiny, far better to meet it taking action than huddled in impotent ignorance.

I dress myself and comb my hair thoughtfully before venturing out. I have been taking more time studying my reflection in the mirror than I hope I spent before losing my memory, on the chance that the familiarity of my face might at least conjure up a name, if not a history. My hair is chestnut brown, thick and somewhat long, my eyes seem to change depending upon the light and colors that surround me, I would wager that I am approximately six feet tall, around thirty years old, and my build is medium. Whether others would find me handsome or not is something I am incapable of assessing. At least I can say that I possess no disfigurations, and for that, I am grateful. It suggests that whatever befell me was not particularly violent.

Then again, perhaps I eluded whatever violence might have been planned for me.

Satisfied that I would not concern the neighbors with my appearance—given that my story was bound to prompt some consternation—I step cautiously outside. The morning is fine and clear, an early spring morning redolent of heady lilac and hollow, cool daffodils. I decide to call on my closest neighbor to my right, whose yard sports a number of signs that at first I had supposed were political, but in fact, turned out to be far more cryptic: "I support the Oxford comma!" read one. "Moles, yes! Gophers, no!" read another. "Today is not that day!" read yet another.

The last one gives me the most food for thought. As I stand on the porch with the worn floorboards slanting ever so slightly to my left, listening to the elaborate chimes that the doorbell produces, I think perhaps it means that this is not the day for us to meet. No one comes to the door, though I ring twice and knock once.

So I decide to try my other next-door neighbor. I retrace my steps past my house, and approach Neighbor Number Two's abode. The houses in this neighborhood, mine included, are Craftsman-style bungalows painted in colorful shades, with deep front porches. This particular house has an eyebrow window built above the porch, giving the house a sleepy, yet watchful look. The steps creak as I mount them, and before I even have a chance to ring the bell, the front door opens. The man who stands before me has a most remarkable placement of hair on his face and head: generous puffs above each ear, thatchy eyebrows that threaten to stab each eye with bristles, and two prodigious wads sprouting

16

from his nostrils. The latter he has obviously attempted to trim and tame, with lackluster success.

"Good morning," I greet him.

"Good morning," he replies guardedly.

"I wonder if I might trouble you this morning?"

"You might."

He makes no move to invite me inside and his lack of congeniality has me wondering how to proceed. "You see, I— I seem to have lost my... well, my memory," I say. This admission prompts a look of startled interest.

"Have you now?" At this point, he steps to one side and sweeps his arm back in an invitation. "Well, you might as well come in," he says. "And have a piece of poppy seed cake."

We walk through his foyer, one graced with an antique hat rack from which a plaid orange cap hangs, along with a mustard-colored rain slicker. An umbrella stand holds a walking stick, a broad sword, and a tennis racket, but no umbrella. From there, he ushers me into his small kitchen, where I gather that he is either of Irish descent or an Hibernophile. No sooner have I noticed the framed photos of dingles and lochs, the green curtains and tablecloth, and a replica of the Blarney Stone sweetly urging me to kiss it than I startle myself for having come up with the word "Hibernophile." How would I know that word? Am I, perhaps, Irish myself?

He puts a kettle on to boil, then removes a cake bell from a cutting board to reveal a plump loaf of poppy seed cake. He cuts us each a thick slice and lays them on small plates, shoving mine over to me across the table. The cake looks and smells dazzlingly delicious, which makes me realize how sparely I have been eating since losing my memory—and if the contents of my refrigerator and pantry are any indication, before that as well.

"May I ask, do you know my name?" I say, when it appears that he is waiting for me to begin whatever trouble my story is going to cause.

He gives a short bark of a laugh as he pours us each a cup of tea. "I don't."

I sigh in frustration. "Why... not?" I decide to ask. "If I may be so bold."

He gives a grim chuckle. Then he sets my teacup before me with a jittering rattle. "You wouldn't tell us. When we— the Welcome Wagon committee, that is—came by with a basket full of goodies, you told us you valued your privacy. And you'd thank us not to disturb it."

My heart sinks at this inauspicious tale. "Did I?"

"Yessir," he says, offering me the sugar bowl. I wonder how I like my tea, whether I take sugar or not, deciding to take a lump and see. For all I know, my preferences have changed anyway.

"How long ago was that?"

He squints as he considers, his eyebrows lowering to the point of covering both eyes, as if they are hiding behind a hedge of brambles. "I'd say... maybe two weeks or so."

"Two weeks. And what is your name, sir?"

"Kyle. Kyle McGillicuddy."

"Pleased to meet you, Kyle," I say, offering him my hand. He takes it, gives me a gruff but neighborly shake. "I'm going by Christopher Seabright."

He nods.

"And I apologize for being so rude before. Did I... by any chance, take the goodie basket?"

"Nossir. And a right shame it was."

"Indeed," I say, wishing I had the contents in my larder right now. I do find it rather hard to believe that my former

18

self was so inordinately fond of sardines, but the number of cans that stock my shelves argues otherwise. I need to go grocery shopping, but I'm feeling so vulnerable that it makes me think that I shouldn't be too visible. Or is that a necessary precaution that had been instilled in me before?

"May I ask—who owned the house before I did?" I take a sip of my tea, happy to discover that I do indeed like a lump of sugar.

"Oh, now—that was the Gartenparten family," he tells me, a glint in his eye that I am having a hard time deciphering. "Do you have a moment?" he asks me, leaning back in his chair and sizing me up. "Because that is a story all in itself…"

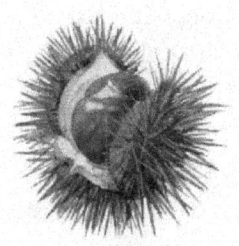

Seconds

Louise Kantro

I can feel Miss Lainie's eyes on me.

We are at the social worker's office and Miss Lainie has asked to talk to me alone.

"You don't have any other relatives besides Harmonia that Social Services could find," Miss Lainie says. It seems like she's asking me a question, but I can't figure out what that question is. We already told them we never met any other family besides Tia Mona, who used to come around only when she was desperate and skinny and should-a been hungry but would never eat anything. (I didn't tell Social Services or the sisters that part.) She and Mami would go off someplace and come back all giggly, and Papa would get mad. Her visits worked out pretty good for her cuz she got to get high that day with Mami and, even if she got a couple bruises from Papa as a bonus, he'd throw a couple of twenties at her (to get her out of the house, I guess), enough for drugs for I don't know how long.

I wouldn't want to dirty the sisters' ears by describing how Tia Mona lives. Sometimes she's so high she don't even close the door when she's doin' some guy, so now Lilia and Cici and I just pretty much stay away 'cept to sleep (and it ain't so easy to sleep, but since we're all together in one room, it's okay). Tia don't keep much food, but there's a little, mostly chips and cookies, and we get breakfast and lunch at school through the free lunch program. Two meals ain't so bad, only some days I get real tired at soccer practice.

21

Ernesto's mom always brings him a snack, and lately she's been bringing me one too, which I have to say I ain't too proud to eat. It's good for the team, right?

When we first moved in with her, I found an old rusty lawn mower in the backyard shed, so I asked her if she wanted me to mow the lawn. She nodded, holding her head still so it wouldn't fall off, I guess, and I figured that since I got permission to use the mower, I could get me some lawn-mowing jobs in the neighborhood. After three weeks, I had seven once-a-week jobs. I covered the whole neighborhood—more than a mile-and-a-half all around—and that's all the jobs I could get, so I decided it would have to do. Lilia, Cici and me, we had to have a little money. I wasn't even going to spend it on food unless we got real hungry. I had to use some to buy some toothpaste and laundry soap. Tia ain't big on hygiene, and we couldn't go to school dirty.

When we were in the hospital, after Mami and Papa left and the sisters came to visit us (they were there every day, sometimes together and sometimes separately), Lilia told me she wanted to go live with Maestra, Miss Joan. She only said it that one time, though. Maybe she thought that wishing would jinx it. Can't blame her for that. None of us could ever figure out how Papa always seemed to know our thoughts. That, of course, was when he'd get out the belt. We learned to not even think when we were around him. We just became completely blank. So I guess Lilia figured that if she thought something too hard, it would become something bad, something that hurt.

The sisters don't get it, though. I know they think they've "been there" for us, and maybe they have, in their own way. But they're so cultured, every hair in place. They just don't know the world we know, just like we never ate off china dishes.

"We got to tell them," Lilia says right before we're going to meet the sisters for lunch. We're waiting for Miss Lainie and Miss Joan behind the restaurant, in the parking lot.

Even if Lilia's right, we ain't gonna tell 'em unless we absolutely have to. I'm the oldest and they gotta do what I say.

Lilia's begging can be obnoxious, 'specially since she knows that even though she's making me mad, she's also getting to me. She's just too scared, all the time scared, but in her own way tough. She used to never talk 'cept to me and Cici, but now she talks a little more.

When I shake my head at her—*no, we ain't gonna tell*—she pulls Cici close to her the way Cici pulls her dolls to her when she plays mommy.

We get through the beginning part of lunch, the stuff we do while we look at the menu, the "OK's" and "Everything fine's" squeezing through our teeth, and we're sparkling with peppermint breath from the Crest we all piled on before we got into our cleanest shorts and tee-shirts.

Miss Joan always includes us all like we're students in her class—real fair and democratic—but when Lilia plops down next to her like she always does at these little lunches, it's clear that Lilia is her favorite. It makes sense, of course, since she was Lilia's third grade teacher and I had Mrs. Parson. Cici is only in kindergarten now and won't have Miss Joan anyhow cuz we don't go to that school no more. I used to be jealous. Even if you can understand a reason, it's hard when you're not liked the best. Then I realized that Miss Joan wasn't my favorite. I like the cop, her sister, Miss Lainie.

We didn't know what to call them when we first met

them. Lilia called Miss Joan *Maestra*—teacher—till finally one of 'em, Miss Lainie, I think, said, "Just call us Joan and Elaine." Well, 'course we couldn't do that, so we settled on Miss Joan and Miss Lainie since Cici couldn't say "Elaine." Everybody else calls her Elaine, she told us, but she really likes the name Lainie. It would be a special name reserved for us.

What I hated the most was how weak I was when they found us. I couldn't hardly move for two weeks. I'm really the strongest, but the day Mami and Papa left us behind, I was the one got kicked and punched before they tied us up.

I thought the hardest part was gonna be going back to school, but I was wrong. The county people told us it was hard to get a place that would take all three of us, and there were all kinds of other kids at the first house. It seemed like it was gonna be fun—there were two boys about my age and I thought we could all play soccer in the street—but nobody was nice and people kept stealing from us. Miss Joan and Miss Lainie kept on coming by (I think that's what started these lunches), and we just pretty much did what we were told. Lilia has always been a good girl. It's harder for me to just go along with things, but I learned real early that, if I ever argue back, I won't be the only one gonna pay the price.

We got moved from house to house. There were four altogether. We always went to school, but different ones whenever we changed foster homes. Our favorite was the Mathesons, but Jim's mother died and he had to go Back East for a while, and seven kids was too many for Mary by herself, so the social worker took us to the Ortegas.

When we had been in the first foster home for about a week, Miss Joan and Miss Lainie invited us for lunch with them at a restaurant. Then at another lunch about six months later, they told us our auntie wanted to be our guardian. "What auntie?" I asked, though I was pretty sure I knew.

"You've met your aunt Harmonia, right? She told the social worker she used to visit your mom sometimes," Miss Lainie said.

I looked at Lilia. Like me, she wasn't showing nothing on her face. Miss Joan and Miss Lainie meant well, but what in the world made them cook this up? Didn't they know about Mona?

It was at this moment that I knew I was gonna have to be watching out for the three of us cuz Miss Joan and Miss Lainie didn't have a clue.

"Mario?" Miss Lainie says, bringing me back to this restaurant, this meal, almost two months since the county put us with Tia Mona. "A penny for your thoughts."

We're sitting at a round table in one of those Denny's-type restaurants near where we been staying with Mona. I chose the place cuz we can walk there, so we been meeting here ever since. Cici is in between Lilia and me, and the sisters are sitting next to each other, Lilia next to Miss Joan, and I'm next to Miss Lainie.

It seems like the sisters been asking to meet more often since we went to Mona's. They ask us every time how we like living with "Harmonia," have the social workers visited the home, stuff like that. Blah-blah-blah. I don't know why we always have to talk about it over and over again. But now we're done with that crap and can talk about other stuff.

"I made the soccer team," I say to answer Miss Lainie's "Wazzup?" (not her exact words). I'm as big as an eighth or ninth grader even though I'm only in sixth grade, but I'm about three inches shorter than Miss Lainie and Miss Joan. They're giants—about six feet tall—only Miss Joan is kind of scrawny and Miss Lainie is buff. I guess that's one of the reasons I 'specially like Miss Lainie. She's curvy (she may be old, but, like my friend Ernesto says, "wimen is wimen"). Miss Lainie's all muscle. You can tell she works out. I seen her one time when I was with my friends and she did her cop thing. Some guy, and he was as big as her, got mouthy with her and started to fling his arms around like he was gonna hit someone. She had him in a lock before he could blink.

We talk about soccer for a few minutes, with her asking me for a schedule and promising to come to my games when she can. I just nod. I don't want her to know how cool that would be cuz maybe she'll just forget all about it even if I do give her a schedule, which makes me wonder if she's just being polite and maybe don't even care about coming to my games. I decide I'll get her a schedule if she asks me about it again. Once means she's being polite. Twice means she's interested.

I'm pretty sure I'm her favorite. But then, where does that leave Cici? I don't want her to have nobody—well, nobody besides Lilia and me. Still, I want Miss Lainie to like me best.

I don't know what-all Lilia and Miss Joan talk about, but Lilia is almost purring. Once in a while one of the sisters asks Cici a question. We sometimes have to help Cici answer. She's not so good at English cuz she just started school. Besides, like Lilia, she don't talk much anyhow.

They're nice ladies, the sisters. But why are they doing this, having us meet them for lunch? Are they trying to teach us manners? Do they just want to know they did the right thing setting up for Tia Mona to be our guardians? She's even trying to "make it permanent."

"She is?" Miss Lainie says.

What? Did I say it out loud—about Tia wanting to keep us?

26

"Mario?" Lilia says, and I can tell she wants me to tell them, but, hey, it was a mess-up that I even said anything.

"Well, that's good," says Miss Joan, looking at Lilia. Lilia is careful with her face. Good girl. If Mona gets her way, it's just for the money. Anyhow, we can just run away, but if we tell the sisters how much we hate it at Mona's, they might squeal on us to the county people.

"Is that what you want?" Miss Lainie asks. She gives me a hard look.

I can't look her in the eye. Because I know that she's noticing (she is a cop), I'm trying to think of something to say to keep her from realizing that I am avoiding the question.

"Did you have another family—one of the foster families—that you liked more?" Miss Joan asks.

These two just don't have a clue. Like it matters what we want.

We all shake our heads. Actually, I did like the Mathesons a little, and I think Lilia and Cici did too. Well, so what? The Mathesons are history.

"Mario?" Miss Lainie says, tilting her head at me, her eyes boring into mine, "do you want Tia Mona to—well, adopt you?"

Talk about one-track mind.

Well, Mona never said the word "adopt."

I just keep my head straight. I won't nod and I won't shake my head. I know it's kind of a lie to not even answer her, so I can't look at her. Can she tell what I'm thinking, what I want? If she can't tell, she's stupid. She don't deserve to be my favorite if she can't tell. But if she does figure it out, we're just gonna have to move again, and it could be even worse in the next place.

"Do you think your aunt would—well, let me see," says

27

Miss Joan, twisting her hands nervously. "It wouldn't be polite for us to—"

"Maybe if we invited Mona and the kids over for dinner?" Miss Lainie says. Sometimes the sisters do that. Finish each other's thought. I get a little lost in their conversations sometimes.

"So we could get to know your aunt a little," Miss Joan said.

Lilia and I look at each other helplessly. Mona don't know what she's gonna do five minutes from whenever. She'd never remember a dinner date even if she agreed to it, which she wouldn't anyhow. The sisters don't understand that druggies like Mona don't go to dinner with high-class people. They just don't, period. They go to McDonalds— that is, if they can come down enough to eat at all.

"I wish we could invite you over for dinner," Lilia says, "but we don't know how to cook."

I shoot Lilia a "Shut up!" look.

Miss Joan sits up straighter than usual. "Maybe you'd like to just show us your rooms?"

Room, not rooms. But of course, she don't know.

"Joanie," said Lainie, "it's not our place to be inspectors."

"Yes, of course," Joan says.

Lilia looks about ready to pop. I catch her eye and shake my head. Thank goodness the sisters ain't looking at her. They're looking at each other.

Cici starts tugging at Lilia's arm that she needs to go to the bathroom, so Lilia takes her. The sisters pay the bill with two twenties, a ten, an a five, leaving it all on the table.

Cici is shivering in her sleep, snuggled against Lilia, but I guess she's only warm on the side that's touching Lilia. On the other side the blanket is riding too high. It's a short blanket, one that doesn't quite cover the two of them. I sleep on the floor, wrapped up in one blanket. We used to all sleep together, but not no more. I'm too big for that bed, and besides, I'm too old to sleep with my sisters.

When we first went to Mona's, she told the social worker I slept in the corner of the living room but that she would be moving soon so I would have my own room. I never once slept on the couch.

"We shoulda made her sleep in her clothes," Lilia says. She is wearing a long-sleeved shirt and pull-on pants we got at the Goodwill last Saturday, but Cici wanted to wear her new nightgown. Now she's cold, and all her clean clothes are in the hamper in the living room cuz Lilia and I did our laundry today at the Laundromat. When we got home, Tia was gone and we started watching TV. As soon as we heard her at the door, we hurried into our bedroom. It has gotten late but not so late that Mona's "company" is gone, so we're stuck in here. Maybe later I can go bring in the laundry basket and we can put on some socks and sweatshirts.

"Bring Cici down here," I say. My blanket is bigger, so I have more room to fold her up inside. We fell asleep that way, warm enough, I guess. The sun shining through the window wakes me up. Lilia is with us on the floor, wrapped up in her own blanket.

When we go out to the kitchen, I see a brand new loaf of bread on the counter and wonder if we should open it. Tia will notice—or will she? Sometimes she has the eyes of a hawk. Other times, the drugs scramble up her brain. I leave the end piece and take out three pieces. "She won't be able to tell," I say, handing the slices to Lilia, who spreads some peanut butter across the tops. She hands one to each of us, and when we're done eating, she washes and dries the knife and wipes our crumbs off the table. While I use the bathroom, she helps Cici pick out clothes and tie her shoes. Then it's their turn for the bathroom. We only flush once, even if we poop, so we won't wake up Tia, but we absolutely have to flush before we leave. The first morning we were here, we didn't flush and Tia was all over us when we got home. She don't hit us, but she's got a really mean Evil Eye.

After school, first thing, I pick up the girls. Then I mow my lawn for the day. After that, we go to a park right next to the school. We try not to get home till six, or till it's getting dark, which lately has been at about five-thirty. If anybody at the park starts looking at us funny, we just leave for a while then go back. Today, we've been at the park the whole time.

"Hey, Tia," I say when we get home, making sure I don't slam the screen door. I'm aiming for *cheerful* today, hoping it won't bug her. You never know.

Turns out she *likes* cheerful today. She is cheerful herself.

"Guess what?" she says. "We're moving."

"Moving?" Lilia says, trying to hide her feelings, which I think I can guess.

I wish I felt a little more *cheerful* about the whole idea of moving—again. What will happen to my lawn-mowing jobs?

Well, if we didn't move too far...

"Tito says there's room for us at his place. He's got him a big house at the corner of Third and Oak, lotsa bedrooms and a big kitchen, a bi-i-i-g kitchen," she adds, and she giggles, losing track of the conversation. Man, is she high

30

today.

"When are we going?" Lilia asks, and I figure she really wants to ask, "*Where* are we going?" and if we'll be going to the same school and also she's thinking about Miss Joan and Miss Lainie, wondering if they already know. She can't ask any of these questions, though, cuz she don't want Tia to give her the Evil Eye.

"Right now," Mona says. "Get your stuff."

I look around to see if there are any paper bags laying around the kitchen, but I don't see any. I ask Tia if we can use the laundry basket for our clothes, and she giggles some more and waves a hand, which I decide means yes.

We pack up and wait, afraid to turn on the TV so Tia won't get a headache. While we wait, I figure out that we're moving today because it's the first of the month and Tia probably didn't pay rent for a while. She seems to be pretty happy about the whole situation, though, which I just don't get. Maybe she really likes this Tito guy.

When Tito comes, we all slide into the backseat of his Chevy and Tia gets up front. She nuzzles his neck while we drive. We pass Lilia and Cici's school, turn left, go down an alley, and stop in front of a really big house.

Wow! No wonder she's so happy. Tia for sure got herself a sugar daddy.

But when we go inside, I know right away why this guy has enough money for Tia and her sister's three raggedy kids.

Tito takes us upstairs, like a proud papa, and shows us two bedrooms, one for me and one for the girls. Yeah, right. I'm not letting the girls out of my sight, but I don't say nothing to him, just make my face look grateful.

He and Tia head downstairs, and I turn to Lilia.

"Okay, you win," I say. "We're gonna call them."

"Tonight?"

31

"Yeah, tonight, after everybody's asleep."

"But we'll wake them up."

"Yeah, well, then we'll wait till morning." But actually, I don't want to wait till morning. I don't even want to wait till later.

"What's that smell?" Lilia said.

"C'mon," I say, putting my hand on her back and giving her a little push. Cici, who was looking out the window of what's s'posed to be my room, comes running over. She almost knocks me over as she puts her hand in Lilia's. It didn't seem like she was listening, but I guess she was.

"Where're we going?"

"To the store," I say.

At least that's what we tell Tia, and then we walk to the school, put money in the pay phone, and call Miss Lainie at the police station (a long time ago she gave me her cop card and said, "I work from four to midnight"). Since it's seven-thirty at night, I figure she'll be at work.

Only she's not there, she's out "in the field" somewhere.

I tell Lilia to look through the phone book, only a bunch of pages have been torn out, including the F's, which is what we need for Miss Joan, because their last name is Fine.

Lilia gives me her "What are we gonna do now?" look.

I grab Cici's other hand. "There's a phone at this store a few blocks from here," I say, so we walk there. It's dark now with only me to protect the girls, but there is no way we're going back to that house.

The pay phone has a phone book that still has the "F's" and I dial the number for "Fine, J."

Miss Joan answers. I almost give the phone to Lilia since she's the one always talks the most to Miss Joan, but then I remember that Lilia don't know what I know. Besides, I'm the one in charge.

"Miss Joan?" I say. "It's me, Mario. I tried to call Miss Lainie, but she ain't there." Damn, I shouldn't-a said that. But actually, it is kind of a police matter, which even Miss Joan will figure out if I can just get the words out.

I explain as well as I can.

"What's the name of this street?" I ask Lilia, pointing at the street sign. "Miss Joan needs to know where we are, she's gonna come get us."

Lilia shakes off Cici's hand, puts it inside mine, and runs to the street sign. "Maryland," she says when she gets back.

I tell Miss Joan we're at the Seven-Eleven three blocks from Roosevelt Junior High, and she says for us to go inside the store and wait for her. Then she says something else, something important, something that makes me want to throw up, not from feeling bad, but from feeling scared. And I don't scare easy.

"She's gonna come get us?" Lilia asks.

I nod.

"What's a meth lab?" Lilia asks after I hang up the phone. I think about how hard it was to explain to Miss Joan why I was so upset, so I finally just have to out and say what I saw at Tito's house.

"They make drugs there," I say, "and it's not a safe place to be."

"How do you know?" she asks, and I tell her about all the pills and the equipment and the smell and how it all suddenly made sense to me why the house was so big and why Mona was so *cheerful*.

"I wonder if the social worker will send us back to the Mathesons," she says, and she squats down to look at Cici. "You liked the Mathesons, didn't you, Cici?" Cici nods. I'm not sure if Cici is nodding to please Lilia or because she means it, but it don't matter. I'm hoping we ain't gonna live with the Mathesons, even though I did like them, but I ain't saying nothing to Lilia yet.

Miss Joan maybe just slipped up or I didn't hear right, but I don't want to mess things up. No point in saying nothing till one of 'em says something for real, a second time. Maybe Miss Joan didn't really mean it when she said she and Miss Lainie been trying all this time, but now... well, there'd be room for us all in this new house they were getting together, and since Mona is our only relative and she's dealing drugs, maybe the county will let her and Elaine— anyway—but she didn't finish her sentence. I'm sure, almost sure, I heard that word *adopt*.

But then, as if she hadn't even said those words, she asked me the name of the street.

I don't want Lilia to be sad or feel like wishing made it not happen. I just figure that, if one of the sisters, either one, says it again, it's gonna really mean something. After all, the Mathesons were our *second* foster family, Miss Lainie asked me for the soccer schedule a *second* time, she came to my *second* game, and we got through to Miss Joan tonight on our *second* phone call.

Oh, and one other thing. When they found us, it was the *second* time of someone coming. First, Miss Joan came and she actually heard us inside from the outside of the house, which was locked. Then Miss Lainie and her cop-partner broke in and found us.

ARBOREAL

LITERARY MAGAZINE

INAUGURAL ISSUE RELEASE

February 15, 2023

1 COPY = 2 TREES PLANTED

Each print copy sold funds two new trees.

NEXT SUBMISSION PERIOD

March 15–April 15, 2023

VOLUNTEER OPPORTUNITIES

contact@arborealmag.com

See the forest for the trees.

ARBOREALMAG.COM

Sorry, Maggie May

Kathryn Tomasko

I live in the house where my brother died. He lives here too.

Not in the traditional sense, of course. I cook meals for two and eat both servings. He says it's my night to do the dishes when it's always my night to clean up. Hard to use soap and water when they go right through you. But he can still manage to hide my car keys and toss pens at me from across the room, so I think it's all bullshit.

Sometimes it is out of his control, though. Like when his face disappears, and he can't make it come back. It might last a week, him just wandering around like the phantom he is. Eventually, I adjust to it. Jake just doesn't have a face this week. And then I wake up one morning and he's there, bright green eyes right where they're meant to be. But even that gig can be bullshit. He says it's always out of his control, and sometimes it is. He still manages to poke his faceless head through the door while I'm in the bathroom—in an attempt to "help scare the shit out of me"—and all his features will melt back into place as he bursts into laughter.

I know he gets bored, and these are the little pieces of paradise he finds in our strange limbo. That's why I cook two meals, set the table for two, toss a blanket over his lap as we watch movies. Sometimes it sinks through to the sofa, sometimes it will settle over his... form. He doesn't have a body, so I don't know what to call it. But I see him and hear him, sometimes feel him. And I let him get away with his age-inappropriate pranks. You might think thirty years would temper that brotherly inclination to tomfoolery. But not even death gets rid of it, apparently.

The house was our parents', but not the one we grew up in. When we were twenty-three, they sold the childhood home to retire in a cheaper neighborhood, farther from the small city where we grew up. It's a sweet little thing tucked into the mountains, just enough space for an older couple to waddle around. Or for a thirty-year-old and her semi-transparent sibling to haunt. The siding always strikes me, dark brown with darker trim and an ancient, wooden, farm-style door which used to be lighter, but time has worn it just as black as the roof. The house is small, dark, but never cramped or uncomfortable. The epitome of cozy, tucked into a meager clearing of maples and oaks with a long, gently sloping driveway. They loved it, for the time they got to spend there.

Mom got sick first. It was sudden and quick compared to what it could have been. Cancer, of course, as it usually is. Ovarian, of all things, but it started to spread. They got it out of her ovaries just for it to be halfway to her lungs. That's what took a while. She wanted to try her best, stay as long as she could. Did all the treatments and changed to some theoretically cancer-fighting diet. There were tumors, there was shrinking, surgeries and chemo, regrowths, and remission. And then she was gone. It was good in the end. She was fragile and sunken, but not as bad as she could have looked. And Dad had been in therapy for a long time, building the framework of coping that would carry him through the rest of his life alone. Who knew it wouldn't be that long?

Jake moved in with them before she passed, under the guise of brawny assistance when in truth he was just waiting it out. Waiting for dad to be alone, when he would really need someone but never say anything about it. Jake thought ahead, moved in before Dad would see it as a pitiful act of charity.

So it was Jake and Dad for a while, Jake working his ass off all day and coming home to a creaky sixty-six-year-old who would nag him for the rest of the night. And he never complained. Well, he'd bitch a little to me over the phone. His back was hurting from hauling lumber and whacking hammers at wood all day (or whatever he did) and Dad would give him a headache now and then. But he loved the house, he loved our dad. He was happy.

I would visit when I could. I'd taken so much time off when Mom was sick that I sort of had to make it up to my boss afterward. She never said so, but I felt it, so I worked myself raw in the office and brought drawings home to work on through the nights. Architecture—sounds so fun on paper, really kind of sucks in practice. At least I like numbers because there's a lot of math and proportion work. I ended up taking a few weekends here and there to spend with Jake and Dad, and there were moments where it felt like nothing had changed. We would sit in the kitchen with stacks of pancakes and exorbitant slabs of bacon, splattering coffee on each other as we laughed with our noses in our mugs. Our laughter filled the little house, and it was so easy to think that mom was just in the bathroom, gone from the table for a minute but sharing the space with us still. I'm glad she was never actually there.

I love sharing the house now with Jake, I really do. It's unheard of and unimaginable and I don't ever have to be without my best friend. But if it was Mom, or if she was there too, my heart would break every day and I'd probably sob uncontrollably, bringing priests and rabbis, anyone spiritual, into the house to help her get out. She wouldn't deserve to be trapped in the wood floors and sheetrock of the house she died in. Jake doesn't deserve it either, but if I lost him, the last piece of my family... Let's assume I'd be walking through the doors without a face too.

Dad had a freak heart attack and that was it. Jake went to work, then Dad was on the couch when he got home. Dark, to say the least. One doctor hypothesized it was all the bacon, which it probably was but also, that must have been some killer bacon because he was pretty healthy. Then this other guy in a white coat who probably just barely earned his M.D. title offered that Dad's heart just couldn't go on without Mom, that it had happened before. If it was meant to make Jake and I feel better, it just made us weep. I hope that's not how they're teaching bedside manner at Johns Hopkins. I wonder if that's something they actually teach. If it's not, maybe they should start.

I stayed with him after Dad's funeral for about a week, a little more maybe. Helped him box stuff up, stock up on food, handle all the legal crap. House was left to him, of course. He'd lived there for the past three years. We mostly spent the days watching our classic stack of go-to movies and arguing over who got which of Dad's coats. The man was spiffy, and we were all the same size. Luckily, he was also neurotic and had an even number of everything from shoes to socks to razor blade refills. Once we'd sufficiently battled over the artifacts of our beloved father, I had to pack up and return to my studio apartment and the plant I was sort of keeping alive.

Then it was just Jake and the House. He called me a lot at first. Every night we'd FaceTime and eat dinner or watch the same movie online. We kept each other company because, in truth, I was just as lonely as he was. My plant began to fade, looking particularly starving, but I never remembered to water it. Jake's back was hurting more and more, but he always refused to take ibuprofen which I never understood. At one point I told him that he surrendered the right to complain about things that he never tried to fix. I'd been half-joking. But I always run the words back and think about how harsh they were. Had I said it with a sneer? Did I raise my voice at him? I can't remember, but I know I said those words and the call fell silent.

After that, we started talking less and less. I chalked it up to returning to routine. My job was booked, Jake's company had won a big project in the city. You'd think that meant we saw each other more, being in the same city, but we didn't. I looked it up afterward. His job was five blocks over from my office. We should have had lunch every day. Things might have been different. But people suck and relationships go two ways and grief is very weird and sticky. We got stuck in these self-destructive routines of work/sleep, work/sleep. There wasn't any self-care in there, as my therapist has said. And she's right, and I understand the concept, and I still don't do it all that much. Self-care is foreign, grief is sticky.

Now it's Jake, me and the house. Jake and I, sharing a bathroom that only I use and staying up all night on the sofa watching movies that would have made our mother shout from upstairs. It's so much the same and so fucking different.

I wasn't scared when I first came home from Jake's funeral to find him sitting at the kitchen table. At first, I thought I was crazy, or I hadn't shaken the hangover quite as well as I'd assumed. I kicked off my waxy black shoes, took the tie out of my jacket pocket, slung everything over the back of the couch. My mouth was packed full of mint gum, but my throat still tasted like vodka, so I figured juice or water, or something would help. And I found him at the kitchen table.

"Hey," he looked up at me, but his eyes didn't meet mine. He looked confused, a little scared. He was wearing a gray shirt and navy sweatpants. He didn't look that bad.

"Hey," I said, a hand on the back of a chair, trying to see if things were real, digging my fingernail into the varnish.

"Um..." he clicked his tongue. "Funeral. Right?"

"Yeah," I sat in the chair. I didn't fall through it to the floor, neither did Jake. So we were real.

"Sorry," he said. And we sat there for the rest of the evening in silence.

The house was mine, bequeathed via his hand-written excuse for a last will and testament. I had read it and reread it a dozen times. His handwriting sucked. How do you get to be thirty and still have those lame little a's that might as well be squashed u's? My brother had never been elegant. When I visited the place in the days before his funeral, it was a wreck, confirming my point. Our aunt came to help clean shit up, cook a few meals, and straighten out the legal crap. Since Mom and Dad died way sooner than planned, the inheritances Jake and I got were pretty substantial. And then Jake gave me his. So I was staying in the house, hadn't gotten rid of my apartment, and was working from home thanks to the undying generosity of my angel of a boss.

The first week after his funeral I decided I was definitely crazy and chose to live with it. After all, was it really so bad to hallucinate my dead brother for the rest of my life? I settled into a bizarre type of mania for ten days, not going to work, obsessing over his phantom, pretending I was ten again and things were okay. We didn't even talk about the fact that he was dead. Didn't address a single thing. Not the note, the rope, not the marble slab that was on its way to the cemetery. We told and retold the same stories, watched all our movies, both of us embracing the most insane denial I've ever experienced.

He broached the subject first. Of course he did.

"I'm dead." It was the middle of Treasure Planet, right at my favorite bit. He looked over at me, same tousled hair and tired outfit as every day. "Maggie, I'm actually dead."

"Yeah," I swallowed, growing lightheaded. The room stretched out from me, I couldn't feel my body. When I spoke it didn't feel like the sounds came out of my mouth. "You made sure of that. You're saying you regret it?"

"I don't know. I think I just realized it though. Really realized." He was staring at his hands, turning them over and pressing his fingertips together. "I don't really feel anything."

I didn't speak. Couldn't.

"You're not crazy, you know. I was waiting around for you to show up after the funeral. Just standing around all morning."

"A hallucination could make justifications for itself," I said.

His mood soured. "Oh, okay, doc. You're an architect, stick to that. I'm the ghost, so I'll speak for ghosts. Don't tell me I'm not real."

"How can you expect me to just... assume you are real. And not think I'm crazy? Mom died, Dad died, I never saw them. You never did either—you would have told me that. But you die, and it's too much, and my brain breaks and now I see you. It makes just as much sense as ghosts. More, if you're a logical person."

I saw him move for the remote to pause the movie, but

he couldn't pick it up. It was like he didn't even try. He snapped into frustration. "Maggie—I'm HERE."

"Okay, well where are Mom and Dad? They died here, too, and you're the only one who's turned their death into a whole thing. I'm supposed to be the one with meltdowns, right? So this is just another one of those." I grabbed the remote and turned the volume up.

"Can you stop!" He stood, hands held tensely before him. Like he'd grab me by the shoulders and shake me till my head fell off if he could. "This is happening to me, too. Get your head out of your ass, alright? You're dramatic but you've never had mental problems beyond fear of public speaking. I'm the nuts one."

I laughed, leaning my arms on my knees, head in my hands. "Sorry, I didn't mean to cop your personality. I know that's your whole thing."

I spent a while staring at him. Same clothes, same hair, the guy I've always known. Standing in the darkened living room, TV flashing behind him. I realized he didn't cast a shadow, and no shadows were cast on his face. He was just kind of there in flat light. His hair didn't even have its usual wave of dark sheen over his forehead. He was like a colored-in Jake outline.

I held out my hand to him. He reached out his. My eyes would swear he touched me, but I didn't feel anything. Not even cold, or warm. He slapped his hand through mine, and that sent a strange electric tingle up a single vein in my arm before fading at my shoulder.

"Weird," I breathed.

"I'm dead, Maggie." He looked heartbroken.

"I know."

He settled beside me on the couch. The cushion didn't move, the springs didn't squeal as they gave under weight.

There was no weight; he wasn't there.

I had to bite my tongue to keep an accusatory barrage from smacking him across the face. He was only dead because he chose to be. It's his fault. I wanted to ask him if he regretted it, or just the fact that he ended up gossamer after the fact. Would he do it again if something in the world could promise him he wouldn't persist once he was in the ground? I don't think I wanted the answers, anyway. I kept my mouth shut. Let the movie play out with neither of us watching, me gnawing off the remnants of my cuticles, and him staring into the visage of his lap. He asked if I was tired, I said I was, and I climbed the stairs to the little guest bedroom. He stayed down there. He didn't ever get tired.

After that, I woke up every morning with 'Jake's dead' being the first thing I thought. Jake's a ghost. An interdimensional fragment of whatever human beings are made of. So, I went from manic denial to an unsettling hyperfocus on what this meant, what he could do. Could he read my mind, or try to possess me? No, but it was funny to watch him try. What happened if he stood right where I stood? Answer: that gross electricity all over my body. He felt no different. He never felt anything. Could he pick things up? No. But then, I absently asked him to pass the creamer one morning and he did. Just pushed it across the table. I didn't notice the achievement until he slapped the tabletop, hard, and it made the slightest sound. Like he'd gingerly placed a bowl of soup down.

"Wow," I remarked. "That doesn't make sense."

He was beaming. "Ha-ha! I can do things! Dude, I haven't moved anything in—seventeen days! Do you realize how much shit you move around with your clunky body? No, you don't. Not until you're a glorified breeze and can't move a thing."

"The sound was so weird," I said, lowering my eyes to the table, rubbing the spot where his hand made contact. "Try it again."

Jake stood, cranked his arm back as far as he could, brought it down quickly and hard. His palm just stopped at the tabletop, made no sound.

"Huh," I turned my head to one side, pressed my cheek against the wood. It seemed like his hand was resting on the surface. But with his flat-light, colored-in appearance, I really couldn't tell. He looked edited into the scene, as though his hand was not only not on the table, but he wasn't in the room at all. Simply projected onto the image after the fact.

"Fuck," his shoulders fell as he slumped into the chair he wasn't sitting in.

"We'll figure it out," I encouraged, knocking my foot forward to nudge him. I only stubbed my toe on the chair's leg. He didn't seem to notice, so I called no attention to it. "So, you're not much of a poltergeist. There are other types of ghosts."

"Are there types?" He lifted his head. I noticed the morning sun shining through the window behind him, shining through his forehead. I squinted against it.

"Yeah, for sure. I'll get some books and we'll watch some movies about it."

"What, like the Paranormal Activity flicks? I'm not a demon summoned by witches, Mag."

"Hm, are you sure?" I closed one eye, pursed my lips. "I dated that Wiccan, remember? Maybe she did some hinky shit. Cursed our family or something."

"Hinky," he echoed, quirking a smile. "She was pretty whacky."

"Eccentric," I said. "Eh, I got out when I needed to."

"Not before she cursed our family name, apparently," he chuckled.

I loved the sound of his laugh. I was so lucky to still hear it. Which aroused a new question—why could he speak all the time and pretend to sit on chairs but not move the creamer on purpose?

He conceded, "Alright, get your books. We'll watch the movies. You'll have to keep a running list of things we're going to test. I wonder if I could make the walls, like, ooze gross material."

"Gross material," I stressed. "As in blood? Bodily matter? Or green ooze like R. L. Stine?"

"Mm, R. L. Stine was in fact a pile of green ooze. But I was thinking nasty, kind of black mold style gunk. You see that a lot in horror movies lately."

"You're not wrong," I nodded, looking up the opening time of our local library, the concept of rot passing through my mind.

Sure, we could google everything. But the library was more fun. Books made it feel like research, an experiment. A demented dissertation. And we could test his poltergeist ability on thin pieces of paper, heavier book covers, stacks of books. It would be nice if we got him to the point where he could read one by himself. "Library opens at eight. That's early."

"Poor librarians," he said.

"What is it now... oh, 8:30. Cool. Want me to leave the TV on? I'll go now and we'll get started." I rubbed my hands together, rather devilishly.

"I wonder if I can come..." his eyes wandered out the front window, down the long drive.

"Not gonna kill you to try," I said, not intending the

joke. But he laughed, so it was fine. "Let's go, Basket Case."

"Shotgun," he called, and it made me wince. At least he hadn't blown his face off. If he had, would he walk around without a face all the time?

I opened the front door, tugging my jacket on as I went. He followed so close I should have been able to feel his heat in the autumn air, seen a hint of his breath. I had to stop thinking about all the stuff that was missing from him. I shook my head and took a deep breath.

He meandered to the car, and it was even weirder to see him outside, in natural light. His whole body looked like a hazy paper cutout slapped on top of some half-baked collage of a half-baked high school artist, with rough-cut edges and too much glue running out from beneath the paper.

"Buckle up," I urged him after opening the passenger door.

"No," he said with all the dogged sass of a five-year-old as he plunked on the seat.

I got in, threw the car into reverse, shaking the thoughts of my dead brother sitting next to me. He wasn't a ghost, we were just going to the library. I hadn't buried him two weeks ago, I was just here for a break. That's all. Just me and Jake in the car.

We both expected him to disappear in a puff of smoke when we reached the property line, so we were edgy. I rolled down the driveway slowly, way slower than was necessary. It was a dead-end road in a retirement town. Not a lot of vehicular dangers. The mailbox came into view in the side mirror. I kept my eye glued to the little red flag, not wanting to look at my brother who wasn't really there, not wanting to watch him fizzle away before my eyes. He was turned around in his seat, baited eyes locked on the asphalt road.

"I can walk around the property," he said, and I jolted

47

the breaks at the edge of the drive. "When you went into Dad's office yesterday to reset the Wi-Fi, I decided to go on the back porch. Then the last step. I walked to the edge of the trees, which isn't that far. But I can do that."

"Good to know," I said. "Um, what—what if this isn't a good idea? I mean, we don't know how it works. I don't know if you're tied here or if I could stuff you in a backpack and take you to Thailand. Like, are you energy strapped to the house, or air that can move wherever, you know?"

"Mm," he nodded, sucked his lips into a flat line. "I don't think it can get any worse, right?"

"You could disappear," I said. "For good."

He knocked his head around, stretching muscles that were buried twenty miles west, six feet underground. "I don't think I would. If I need the house, I'll probably just fall out of the car, right? If I don't need it, I can go anywhere. In theory."

"You were never much of a scientist," I said.

"Well, I'd been thinking about changing up the old career."

"Okay," I pulled my foot from the break and let the car roll onto the street.

"Actually," he stopped me before our seats breached the property line. "It's kind of freaking me out. Maybe we can try another time..."

"You sure?" I asked, my heart slowing to its normal pace.

"Yeah," he flashed that grin, the one that meant things were off. "I'll be fine. Maybe I'll walk out to the trees again. Stick a leg past the trunks and see if it falls off."

"Sounds like a plan," I nodded. "Besides, I'd look pretty nuts talking to myself in the library aisles, right?"

"Oh, insane. Especially in the age of Bluetooth." He went to open the car door. His eyes slimmed and, instead, he just moved through it. I couldn't explain how it looked no matter how hard I tried. With every dictionary and thesaurus at hand, no combination of words can really encapsulate the visual of my colored-in brother phasing through metal and glass.

I tossed him a wave and wheeled onto the road, not speeding but also a little quickly. He stayed in the rearview mirror, watching me go. I wanted to bring him with me so bad. I also wanted him to stay in that house and never go anywhere again. I wished he wasn't a ghost, wasn't dead, or at least the kind of dead that didn't stick around. But then, I never wanted him to go anywhere else ever again. I was able to stifle my violent sobbing as I reached the library parking lot, though my eyes and cheeks must have been blearing red and puffy as I walked in.

The library was small. Cozy, like everything in this minute town seemed to be. As if retired folks didn't require much more than five-hundred developed square feet around them at all times. The roads could have been one way without causing any issues. I doubted these people went many places at all. We had gone out for supper once, right after Mom and Dad bought the place. Years ago, now. Our pack of four was accompanied only by the waiter who was also the busboy, a lazy manager behind the register, and an ancient man sitting in one corner taking his sweet time on a bowl of French onion. We had giggled at it. Growing up in the city set Jake's and my social/spatial awareness at such a resting high that we must have looked wired, strung out. Always looking over our shoulders only to see the manager had fallen asleep.

The building's green-painted metal door slammed behind me, startling the librarian behind the counter who was shockingly young. As I flashed a sheepish grin, she smiled to reveal some sweet, early crow's feet. I clocked her at about thirty-five, wondering if she drove from a town or two over for this sleepy job in this older-than-dirt town. She was cute, too, but I kept it to myself as I took in her conservative, rather unimaginative clothes. She lifted her eyes from a dinosaur of a desktop (the fat white kind) to greet me with a smile as she pushed her deep green glasses back on her nose. I wondered if she had picked the door's paint color.

"Wow, good morning!" Her voice was sprightly and fresh. Maybe she was closer to thirty-two.

"Wow, hello," I matched the energy of her grin.

"Sorry, no one gets here till..." she glanced at the clock-face on her wrist. "Eleven-thirty? The oldies come in then, and I've yet to see any of the younger ones around."

"Are there younger ones here? I thought 'retirement town' was just a phrase. Like, if you retired there personally, it was your retirement town."

"Well, it's called Homestead. That's pretty buy-a-house-and-die-there isn't it?" She laughed, and it was pretty. But my stomach lurched. "What's a twenty-something doing here?"

"Visiting my brother," I said, genuinely not believing the words as they came out of my mouth. It wasn't wrong, but it still tasted like a lie. "I'm looking for some books on ghosts. Not paranormal fiction but more..."

"Historical? We have some local lore books... Hold on." She tapped away at the clunky keyboard, loud clacking smacks that made me blink every time she slapped them.

"I mean, do you have informational stuff? I'm kind of... studying up."

"Are you a writer?" Her brown eyes brightened,

50

widening behind her thick-framed glasses.

"Uh, yeah," the least convincing sounds came out of me. But she was helping me lie to her, might as well go with it. "Staying here for the environment, you know? Working—" what do I say here? "On a manuscript." Pretentious ass.

"Oooh, very cool. Lemme see what we have for you. I'm Jean by the way." She held her hand out over the desk.

"Maggie," I shook her hand.

After some typing and scrolling, she pulled out a sticky note, scribbled a few books down, and peeled it off the stack. "So, the closest we really have is some first-account type books. I wrote those here," she pointed with her pen. "And there's this one, Researching the Paranormal. Sounds like it could help. They're all actually logged in our fiction section. Don't really have enough for an 'informative' ghost section. You could probably find lots more online."

"Did you really just tell me not to use books? They should revoke your library card." I tutted and shook my head.

Jean leaned over the counter, a wicked smirk on her face. "I don't even have one. I just take what I want and bring it back whenever." She was pretty cute.

"Wooow. Thanks for letting me know what kind of person you are, you delinquent. But, uh," I leaned in, "I don't have a library card either. So... I'll see you in a few weeks?"

She giggled, shrugged, and reclined back in her office chair. "Sure, Maggie. I trust you. Just give me your address so I know where to send the bill when you 'forget' to bring them back."

"My pleasure," I cocked a grin and snatched the sticky notes. "Here," I handed a slip to her. "My number's there, too. Feel free to verbally harass me until I return them. Because I hate to admit it, I'm really forgetful. You'd be lucky to see my face again."

"I would," she spun back and forth, chewing on the end of her pen. Cute.

"Alright, I'm gonna grab these, and I'll get out of your hair," I pushed off the counter, scanning the labels on the ends of bookshelf rows to the left.

"I'd invite you to lunch, but you're here so damn early," she called as I reached the first fiction aisle.

My cheeks were hot as I barely looked over my shoulder. "Next time," and I watched her nod with a roll of her eyes and a smile. When the silence shifted from uncomfortable to normal, I found myself reaching for my phone to text Jake. His phone was in the house, but I had shoved it into a box with his note and shoved that under the couch. It wasn't ideal, sitting beneath me all the time. But I couldn't go into the bedroom, or I'd huck it onto the top shelf in the closet where I would never reach it. I dialed the house phone instead, giving it a shot. I could leave a message he would hear at the very least.

The familiar, guttural trill of my parents' ancient landline rung about six times, then—"HELLO?" The voice was pronounced but distant.

"Jake...?"

"I smacked the phone off the wall, so I'm lying on the floor. Can you hear me?"

"Yeah," I dragged my finger along the spines of dirty, old dust covers. Now and then the cold metal shelf would hit my wrist like the spit of a knife. "It's weird though. But I think that's only because you don't actually have vocal cords."

"Oh, yeah," his voice almost sounded normal with the upturn of naïve realization. "How's the book trip going?"

"Fine. Librarian is cute."

"Get her number Maggie May," he giggled. My heart

broke. He hadn't called me that in years.

"Already gave her mine. And the address. So she knows where to send the bill for all these books I'm not going to return."

"You know that's theft of public property. Or town property, something like that. Fucked up, dude. What if some little kid needs the books you're getting for school?"

"Mm, they do have a premiere ghost-hunting school in this part of the mountain valley." I pulled two off the shelf, same author. Poltergeist activity and a ghost-basics book, Ghost Hunting for Dummies, essentially. Next one would be on the bottom shelf, so I squatted down. "Why are we doing this again?"

"What else are we gonna do?" he asked.

"Hm." The prospect of searching for a fix dawned on me. We were supposed to be trying to help him to the other side? Find some light or a tunnel? I didn't want to do that. I couldn't live here reading ghost books all day either. "Jean told me to just Google stuff. We should research the old-fashioned way with a classy James Wan marathon."

"Jean? The librarian? Oooooh, first name basis Miss Maggie Dufresne. You're the biggest slut to walk this town's little streets."

"Yes, I am. Proudly. At least I know how to get some, poozer." A weird nickname we spat out when we were five. Never shook it. "Alright, I got these books. It's only three—really abysmal selection. I'll be home soon."

"Step on it because the phone's gonna be buzzing. I don't think I can get it back on the receiver."

"Got it. I'll take my time and be safe. See you in forty." I hung up, readjusted the books on my hip, and headed for the door. I couldn't quite escape Jean's perky goodbye, a telling upturn of her chin as she scanned me up and down.

"See ya never," I flashed a wink and smiled. She was giggling as the door bashed closed behind me.

The Satin Gunmetal Sky

Shawn Goodman

Chapter One

The lights in the diner gleamed off the exposed metal on Schneider's face, cheekbones like razor blades. He was unique even among synthetics, the only one in New DC who wasn't trying to pass. He'd climbed out of the uncanny valley and gone right back in.

Schneider sniffed the air—frying bacon and hot coffee—and strode across the checkerboard floor. He moved smooth and easy, cutting an elegant figure in old-fashioned wingtips, a trim black suit, and wool fedora. Like a jazz musician from the 50s.

He scanned the restaurant, taking in everything and giving back nothing. His eyes weren't empty, but they were on the dark side, just a few clicks to the left of the dial for warmth. He chose a stool three spaces down from the diner's only other customers, a pair of bikers.

One of the bikers, a giant of a man ready to explode out of his leathers, more fat than muscle, glanced over. A double take at the metal showing on Schneider's face. "Fucking synth," he muttered.

The waitress shot the biker a look of warning and turned back to Schneider. She filled his cup with coffee, and said, "hi hon. The usual?"

"Add a chocolate malted to the order, will you, Bev?"

Schneider said.

She grinned. "Celebrating, Detective Schneider?"

"It's my birthday." Bev rewarded him with a laugh.

The biker swiveled on his stool. "Hey, freakshow. Synths don't have birthdays."

Schneider took a sip of his coffee. The biker waited for Schneider to respond, and after a moment, he did. "Did you call me freakshow because I'm a synth, or because I ordered a milkshake for breakfast?"

Bev picked up her carafe and moved quickly down the counter. She topped off the bikers' mugs and said, "shut up, you two, and eat your food."

"Come on, sweet thing," the giant's buddy said. "You don't have to talk to him when there's real men around."

Schneider could feel them trying to gauge his reaction. He remained impassive, watching the cook work the grill with the long edge of his spatula. On the upstroke, he spread a ribbon of oil and cracked Schneider's eggs, two over medium.

The bikers kept at it with Bev. "What time do you get off?" the bigger of the two said. "We'll give you the ride of your life."

"No thanks."

Schneider watched her wipe the already-clean counter.

"Don't worry," the giant said. "It won't be both of us at once. We're gentlemen. We'll take turns." His buddy snorted in place of a laugh.

Bev sighed. She started to move away.

"Hey." The giant leaned over the counter and grabbed at her. "Don't be rude. I'm not done talking to you."

Bev jerked her arm back. A sluice of coffee escaped the carafe and splattered the wall brown.

Schneider took his empty coffee cup and turned it

upside down. He stood up. "It's time for you two to leave."

The giant straightened to his full height—six-five in his Chippewa boots—and faced Schneider. His buddy, a half-head shorter but just as fat, got to his feet as well.

"Are you telling us we don't belong, synth?"

"Or you can apologize. But it'd better be sincere."

The smaller one clicked open a lockblade. To his buddy, he said, "I think he needs a lesson."

Bev started to speak, but Schneider held up a hand. "No, it's okay." He turned and stepped to the door.

The one with the knife said, "smart move."

Schneider kept talking. "I should know better than to think two assholes like you could understand civility."

He flipped the cardboard sign on the door from "open" to "closed," and then locked the bolt.

Chapter Two

Franco knew he was fucked the moment the L.T. called his name. The old bastard shouted it across the precinct like a one-word accusation. Like a curse.

"Franco!" Sound of gravelly, eternally-pissed off voice rolling over the half-dozen tanker desks like a thundercloud. "My office. Now."

Franco started his walk of shame, past his co-workers, each burdened with six months of paperwork and their unit's ever-growing list of unclosed homicides, both human and synthetic.

"Give him hell, Franco." Joe Dixon, hypertensive and bloated from years of stress eating—a meatball sub, 32 oz. Coke, and onion rings his favorite—leaned into the aisle and swatted Franco on the ass.

The L.T. leaned against the windowsill. "Don't bother sitting down."

"Sure thing, boss." Franco pulled up a chair and made a show of unbuttoning his jacket. Settled himself delicately, beefy forearms on the adjustable armrests. He waited for the bad news.

The L.T.'s right eye twitched. "That right there is why no one wants to ride with you."

"What, because of how I sit?" He swiveled the chair back and forth, and then tested the spring mechanism. It groaned like death.

"Because I specifically told you not to sit."

Franco grinned, getting back to his feet. "I'm just messing around, boss."

"You rub people the wrong way, Franco. With you, everything's a pissing match."

"You think I should take it down a little?"

"You should dismantle it. It's fucking exhausting, Franco. You're exhausting."

"You sound like my wife."

"And do you listen to her?"

Franco shrugged.

"You heard of Schneider, from the 14th?" the L.T. said.

"The synth Detective who shot that kid on the Dirty Boulevard? It's been all over the news."

"He's been cleared of charges," the L.T. said. "You should know that the kid—who was 24, I might add—was carrying two automatics."

"Okay, but what's it got to do with me?"

This time it was the L.T. who grinned. "He's your new partner. Starting this afternoon."

"Wait." Franco leaned forward. Didn't see it coming, though he should have. "No way."

58

"I'm not asking for your opinion."

"This is because of what happened in the Bakerman case, isn't it?"

"Yes!" The sergeant waved his hands in circles around his head. "One-hundred percent, unequivocally, it's because of the Bakerman case. Because of what you did to Mr. Bakerman, and all the ass kissing I had to do to fix it."

"Lieutenant. This isn't—"

The L.T. folded his arms. Case closed.

Franco stood and buttoned his jacket. "So what you're saying is, because this Schneider character is such a colossal screwup no one will partner with him. And you're asking me to take him under my wing and—"

"No. No one will partner with you, you big, thick-headed animal! I'd fire you in a minute if the union didn't have your back. Six months of probation was a gift."

"Okay," Franco said after a moment of fabricated consideration. "I'll do it, but just because of the special relationship we have."

"Get out."

Chapter Three

The Dirty Boulevard was steaming its way through the hottest part of July. The 500 block was a study in concrete, soot-covered bricks, and iron-barred windows that bled rust all the way down to the sidewalks, which were littered with cigarette butts and discarded scratch tickets. Half the shops were boarded, but they were still open for business. In lieu of signs, there was spray paint on particleboard, some of it quite artistic. Quality guns and quick background checks. Bail bonds. Number One Relaxing Massage! Boulevard Beer and Liquor Land. Cheapest cigarette prices allowed by law.

Schneider sat in the passenger's seat smoking an unfiltered, his metal forearm resting on the open windowsill. He felt his new partner staring at him, the way most humans did. Twenty percent curiosity, eighty percent disgust. He felt the questions bubbling up. The ones every human asked even though they'd heard the answers before. Do you sleep? Can you feel pain? Are you able to have sex? Yes, yes, and you'd better believe it. And the biggest question of all was about his lack of skin, which was unusual even among synthetics.

"We may as well get this over with," Schneider said. "Go ahead and ask."

"Ask what?" Franco touched the monitor, pretending to scan incoming calls. There were none.

"You know." Schneider blew out a plume. It soaked into the filthy headliner. "Why I had my skin removed." He tapped the metal on his forearm to illustrate.

"The thing is," Franco said, "I don't care."

"Really?" Schneider adjusted his Ray Bans on his gleaming alloy nose.

"That's right. Not interested."

"Maybe we'll get along after all."

Franco scowled. "Let's get this straight, Schneider. If you do your job and stay out of my way, I don't care who or what you are. Skin, no skin."

"I salute your open mindedness."

They rode in silence past a series of anti-SRA billboards of increasing amplitude. The first sign said, "HUMAN is HUMAN," followed by an American flag with the slogan, "UNITED STATES OF NO SYNTHETICS!" The last said, "VOTE NO," referring, of course, to the upcoming Synthetic Rights Act, which promised a substantial upgrade.

Not quite on par with human rights, but several steps up from the basement. Most important to Schneider was Article 6, which would change synth homicide from property crime to actual homicide.

Franco jerked the car around a delivery truck and skidded to a stop in an alley. The walls had been visited by an illiterate graffiti artist. Fuk and Basturd appeared in neon balloon letters, a testament to the Boulevard's less-than-stellar public high school. The cruiser's engine cut to a soft electric hum. "All right, then," he said. "What's the deal with you not wearing your skin?"

"I thought you said you didn't care."

"I don't, but what do you think is going to happen when we show up on cases?" Franco's neck was roped with muscle and veins. The button on his collar looked ready to pop. "What are the vics and families going to say when they look at you?"

Schneider adopted a sarcastic tone. "Yes, what about the other cops?" He covered his mouth with a hand. "What will they think? What will they say?"

"Exactly."

Schneider pointed at the sleeves of his new partner's shirt. "Rather hot out to be wearing a long shirt, don't you think?"

"So? It's a fucking uniform."

"The uniform includes both short and long sleeves. It's 92 degrees. So, either you're hiding needle marks, scars, or tattoos."

Franco said nothing.

"You don't look like a cutter. And since I've never met a 200-pound Italian detective with a heroin problem, I'm guessing tattoos."

"Sherlock fucking Holmes."

"Full sleeves?"

"That's my business. Now answer my question."

"I am. I'm working up to a metaphor here. Why so many tattoos, Franco?"

Franco's face reddened. The man code had a rule about conversations like this. Conversations with self-reflection, and, worse, metaphors. But there was no way out. "Each one says something about me. About who I am as a man."

"There you go."

"What do you mean, there you go?"

"Whatever those tattoos say about you, it's important enough to sweat through that shirt six months of the year. You're willing to make that sacrifice."

"So what?"

Schneider tapped the titanium plating of his forearm. "This says something about me, too. Who I am as a man. I won't cover it up with faux skin that's been grown in a fucking petri dish. I'm done trying to fit in, trying to pass. And I don't give a shit what you or anyone else in the department thinks about it."

"Okay. I get it."

"Good."

"Except you said who you are as a man. You're not a man."

Schneider grinned, the impossibly delicate, segmented metal and silicone of his lips forming the requisite curves. "That's not what your wife said."

Franco didn't hesitate. With the back of his knuckles, he rapped Schneider on the bridge of his nose. Schneider's head snapped against the headrest, knocking the Ray Bans off his face. His fedora tilted askew.

"Say that again." Franco jutted his chin. "I dare you."

Schneider rubbed his face. Underneath the metal, a

hybrid fascial layer dense with sensory neurons. "Touchy?"

"I am when it comes to my wife and family. Nobody talks shit about my family."

Schneider reached for his sunglasses.

"Car 110, what's your location?" The radio cut in loud and sharp.

"Why do they still bother asking?" Franco restarted the car and jerked it into gear. "They know exactly where we are."

"This is car 110," Schneider said to the monitor. It was one of his favorite parts of the job. Just like in the old cop movies, his favorites being The French Connection, and The Departed. He's seen them each a dozen times. "We're heading North on Porter."

The dispatcher gave the code for a dead body, and the address, which happened to be on the 1500's block of the Dirty Boulevard. Close. The official name was Doherty Boulevard, but no one had called it that for twenty years. Not since the factories closed, and large numbers of synthetics moved in, which resulted in the blocks and neighborhoods encompassing and surrounding the Boulevard being dubbed Synth City.

"I know the place," Schneider said. "Red light section. It's above Gabriel's Sex Shop."

"Wonderful." Franco cranked the wheel and hit the gas. "Death and dildos."

*

The smell of synthetic blood wasn't something you ever got used to. The scene at 1536 Doherty was a full-out assault on the senses. Like what you'd get if a surrealist painter went to work with limbless corpses, ocher blood, and spoiled meat.

"Jesus." Franco breathed into his shirt collar, and coughed.

"What'd you think it was going to smell like?" The landlord, resplendent in an undershirt and an unsuccessful combover, pulled his key from the lock. He let the door swing open.

"Going in." Schneider made an abrupt shift in the way he carried himself. He was surprisingly quick. He skirted the bodies—two of them, center of the living room—and slid into the kitchen. Back in the living room, he kicked the bed and bathroom doors open, and checked a utility closet. "Clear." He slipped his gun in his shoulder holster and looked at the bodies, which had been laid side by side on a blanket. And under that, a sheet of 6mm black Visqueen.

"Oh, no." The landlord reeled back from the doorway, shaking his head. "I don't need to see this. This has got nothing to do with me—"

Franco touched his phone and requested backup, then clamped a hand on the landlord's shoulder. A firm squeeze. "Don't even think about going anywhere. When the uniforms arrive, you wave them into the apartment. Tell them we're inside. Got it?"

He nodded miserably.

Franco joined his strange new partner, who had snapped on gloves and was already working his way around the bodies. They were naked. The male was well-muscled, skin shaved smooth with pierced nipples. The female had long red hair and large breasts. Her body was lithe, like a dancer's.

"You see this?" Schneider pointed at the amputations, which looked clean, and skillfully done. Minimal blood loss, which itself spoke volumes about the killer and his method. Most of what they saw on the Boulevard was crude. Hack jobs that spoke of desperation and rage. But this was different.

"Where's the arms?" Franco regretted the words as soon as they came out of his mouth. Stupid questions deserved stupid answers, but Schneider just shrugged. He was too busy studying. Looking at the same things from different angles, hovering his fingertips over surfaces, letting them touch down ever so lightly. His body still, observing the balance between calm and alert. Beyond the room, in the street, sirens howled their way toward them.

"What I mean," Franco continued, "is who takes four fucking arms?"

"What you really mean is, who takes four synthetic arms?" Schneider dipped a swab in a small pool of blood beside the male body. Much of it had soaked into the blanket, but the tight weave of the fabric preserved a skein on the surface. He did the same for the female, avoiding altogether the dark patch of the blanket between them, which was likely cross contaminated.

"Right." Franco pricked his ears to the pounding of boots in the hallway. He moved to the door and filled the frame with his bulk, ready to slow the flow of uniforms into the small space of the crime scene. He let the forensic guys through, then raised his hand in front of a slick-looking man in a tailored, summer weight suit. "Hang on a minute, Carter," he said.

Detective Derrick Carter lowered his gaze to focus on Franco's thick forearm. His eyes radiated distaste. "Move."

"Sure. As soon as you say the magic password." Franco flashed his worst smile, and waited.

Chapter Four

Elizabeth rinsed the salt and bitter liquid from the eggplant slices. A song from an old Tom Waits album played softly in the living room. Rain Birds. She patted the eggplant slices dry and plunged them into a bath of egg and milk.

"I'm close, Louis. It's going to work this time." She'd been talking to the dog throughout her preparation of the meal, in the manner of people who have lived alone for too long.

The dog was an enhanced lab named Louis—one of the very last who had survived the modifications that resulted in, among other things, extension of lifespan. Louis looked out a Lexan bubble installed in an East facing window. Elizabeth had it put in when he'd developed arthritis in his hips; it gave panoramic views of both the street and the yard.

"You disapprove of the killing, I know." She suspended a slice until the excess egg dripped back into the bowl. Then dredged it in a mixture of bread crumbs, freshly ground pepper, salt, and parmesan cheese.

Louis pulled his head from his plastic bubble and looked at his owner with sad, intelligent eyes.

Elizabeth settled the eggplant slices in a pan of olive oil and checked the pot of water, which was not quite roiling. She added more salt. Louis ambled over to the kitchen where he stood waiting.

"I know what you're thinking," she said. "But the deaths are an artifact of the process. A few more tweaks, my Labrador friend, and the survival rate will rise dramatically." She flipped the eggplant slices, which had crisped perfectly.

She held out two pieces of dry pasta. "Which would you like? I have bucatini, and angel hair."

The dog sniffed both, and chose Bucatini. He ate it in two crunches.

*

Elizabeth hummed along to the music while finishing the meal. She set out two bone china plates, layering each with pasta, al dente, topped with a ribbon of homemade sauce. And on top of that, three slices of eggplant with melted mozzarella.

Louis riffled the air through his great nose. He looked up at Elizabeth, as if to say, it smells so good. Elizabeth set the dog's plate on the mat, and poured a splash of wine in his bowl. After that, she sat down with a plate and, absently, flipped through the folder of this week's research. Keven, her assistant, had printed the copies in advance.

The dog devoured the food in quick bites, stretched, and then sprawled on the floor. Elizabeth tasted her eggplant and pushed it aside. Her mind was too busy for her body to eat. Filled to overflowing with arguments and counter arguments.

"I dislike the killing, too," she said, this time more to herself than the dog. "But people should understand. Complicated surgical procedures take years to perfect. How many deaths before Rohman perfected the heart bypass? How many sacrifices before Ray succeeded in performing neurosurgery on a conscious patient?"

Louis struggled to get up, and returned to his Lexan bubble. His forepaws were arthritic, and the transition from lying to standing was especially painful.

"Come on." Elizabeth rose and grabbed a jacket. "Let's get some air. I'll eat later."

The dog turned around and, stiffly, followed his master

out the door.

Chapter Five

Schneider sleeved the swabs, and tucked the package in his jacket pocket. Ordinarily he'd have logged them as evidence. Chain of custody and all that. But the A-Team had arrived, and Franco was enthusiastically starting a pissing match with Carter and Rubin, who were undoubtedly the most ambitious detectives in the New DC Police Department, if not the best. Franco had stretched his arm across the doorframe, effectively blocking the newcomers from entering.

"Move your goddamned arm." Carter unfastened the button of his blazer. Presumably ready for action despite his reputation as a talker, a diplomat. His partner, Rubin, edged closer, his face red with rage.

"Magic password, please." Franco studied his arm barricade, brushed lint from the sleeve. He was a model of patience and equanimity. Behind him, Carter and Rubin boiled. "Get out of the way, you dumb meathead fuck—"

Abruptly, Franco dropped his arm and cleared out of the way. Carter and Rubin were left standing, puffed up with rage and frustration. Franco was all smiles. "Come on in, guys. I was just messing around."

"You're a real asshole, you know that?" Rubin eyed him with menace, but once inside the apartment, he shed the emotion and let the job overtake him. He looked around and smelled the sweet and sour aroma of synth corpses marinating in the summer heat. He knelt by the female body and snapped on gloves, while his partner kept his distance. Carter, the fussier of the pair, didn't like to get his hands dirty if he could help it. Instead, he strolled through the apartment, letting his gray eyes linger on the bookcase, an off-color patch job that had been applied to the drywall, and a single orchid in a glass vase.

"Second time someone's told me that today," Franco said.

The forensic techs laughed inside of their Tyvek smocks as they bustled about, setting up their miniature scanning drones. Carter and Rubin had never given the techs their due respect—calling them lab fleas as often as not—and even this little bit of payback was welcome. As soon as the uniforms and suits cleared out, the techs would activate their devices. Half an hour of run time to capture and stratify all the data that was to be had. Six times out of ten, cases were closed in this manner. Data analysis over real detecting. It had made some detectives lazy, but not the ones at 1536 Doherty.

"What's with the tin man?" Carter buttoned his jacket and checked the pleats on his slacks. They were still as sharp as a cutting edge.

"My new partner. Schneider, meet Derrick Carter and Javier Rubin."

Schneider tipped his fedora at the A-Team detectives. No hard feelings about the tin man comment; as one of the few synthetic homicide detectives, he was used to it. As the only one with metal in place of skin, he'd come to expect it. "Either of you highly trained law enforcement professionals know what we're dealing with here?"

Franco stood back and crossed his arms. He didn't know Schneider's style, but it looked like he was playing dumb. Fishing around to see if the A-team had any info and, if so, would they give it up.

"You tell me." Carter stared unabashedly. "You and

Stallone over there were first on the scene. I'm assuming you checked out the other rooms, and took your time examining the bodies. What do you think?"

"Not much, beyond the obvious." Still playing it close.

"Humor me. Define obvious."

Schneider commenced pacing the bodies, ticking off details as he made his way around. "Victims are both synthetic, physically attractive, mid-twenties for their minted age. Who knows how old they really are, but we'll get their production numbers and run it through the Registry. And they live here, which means they're most likely sex workers. No signs of forced entry, so it's got to be a John or someone they knew. The apartment's cheap, but clean, and filled only with women's clothes. The guy lives elsewhere."

Rubin crouched and touched the left-arm incision of the female. "Looks very clean."

"Whoever did this has medical experience." Franco moved in for a closer look. "Or he's a butcher. Or a hunter."

"Who hunts anymore? Cuts look medical to me." Carter checked inside the cavities: mouth, ears, nostrils. He inspected the genitals, which were intact, and without obvious trauma. "I'm going with a disgraced doctor, or surgical tech."

"So, we've got a psycho with medical experience who's targeting synthetic sex workers." Franco looked around the room. "And he's doing what with them? Taking their arms for what purpose?"

"Souvenirs." Rubin wasn't sure, though. Just throwing it out there, which was common practice at this early stage. The equivalent of a brainstorming session in the business world.

"No. Not souvenirs." Schneider seemed disappointed. He drifted toward the front door. Time to go.

Franco eyed his new partner but made no move to follow. "Hair and teeth and jewelry make good trophies. They're small and last forever. Two pairs of arms? Not so much."

"Bigger, heavier, and more cumbersome than you'd think," Schneider offered, his hand on the doorknob.

"He could put them in a freezer," Rubin added.

"It's not intimate enough. The killers and mutilators usually want intimate." Franco started to catch Schneider's drift. They weren't going to learn anything new by staying here. Any further speculation would be unproductive in moving the case forward. It would serve only to lighten the cloud of frustration that hung over this part of most homicide investigations—especially considering that the unknown to known ratio was easily thirty to one.

Carter and Rubin exchanged a glance. Some connection flickering between them.

"What?" Franco stopped short of the door.

"It's like the other one," Rubin said.

"Which other one?"

Carter shot his partner an accusatory glance.

Schneider approached, suddenly interested—in both the case and the meaning behind the glance.

"Brooke Marquise," Rubin said. "About six months ago. She was like this one here, a synthetic. Sex worker."

"Missing her arms? Why didn't you say so?"

"Not her arms. One leg."

"Above or below the knee?"

Carter tapped his thigh. Not wanting to have this part of the conversation, but now obliged.

"How come we didn't hear about this?"

"Because it's closed."

"And?"

"What don't you understand about it's closed? The perp was a weaselly little perv named Pelletier. Blind in one eye. Had a thing for amputees."

"You liked him for it?"

"What's not to like? It was a full confession. You should have seen the guy's house. He had these fake arms and legs—what do you call them?"

"Prosthetics."

"They were all over the place. Metal ones, carbon fiber ones, even some old antiques made from wood and plastic."

Franco grunted. "Sick fuck." The hatred of criminals—especially perverts and child molesters—was, after all, common ground for every cop. It was their sacred patch of dirt, and Franco enjoyed scuffing his boots in it as much as the next guy.

"You got that right. Crazy bastard didn't make it one week in prison." Rubin ran a finger across his throat.

Schneider nodded and headed for the door. Franco watched him and noted the faintest trace of a limp. He tucked the observation away, for later.

Chapter Six

Franco raged down the hallway, dragging Schneider by the arm. When they were safely out of earshot of the other detectives, he said, "What the hell was that? We weren't done in there."

Schneider brushed off his hand. He leaned back against the wall, arms folded and one slim leg crossed over the other. "I got the idea you didn't trust them. I was acting on that."

"I don't trust them, but I wasn't finished. I didn't get to look at the bodies."

"We've got all we need."

"My ass we do."

"Did you notice her hair?" Schneider waited a second.

"Yeah, it was red. Like, dyed red."

"It was arranged. Smoothed out."

"So?"

"So, that, in combination with the fact that there was very little blood, means the victims were killed somewhere else, and brought to the apartment."

"Okay, so it's staged."

"Maybe. Or maybe he didn't need them anymore and was simply returning them. Or getting rid of them. Or getting rid of the parts of them he no longer needed. But the point is, he's careful. Very careful."

"Okay, but again, we knew that already. From the cuts."

"And he's unemotional, except that he treated them with respect. Does respect count as an emotion? No, I don't suppose it does." It wasn't clear if Schneider was talking to Franco or to himself.

Franco's thick features drew together as he thought about this. "That's still nothing."

"There's two more things. First, the blanket."

Franco was keeping up with him now. "I saw it. Must be new because it's got creases in it, like it just came out of its wrapper. Which means he brought it with him. Which means, what? He wanted to make them comfortable?"

"Maybe. And you want to make people comfortable when you care about them in some way. Could be a romantic kind of caring or something different."

"That's a weird way to show you care, by cutting off arms."

Schneider was lost in thought. "He must have needed those arms very badly."

73

"Whatever."

"What could you do with two pairs of synthetic arms?"

Franco shook his head clear. "You said two things. What else?"

"She had a jade plant in the kitchen. It was wilted, but she had it propped up with sticks, like she was trying to save it."

Franco cracked his knuckles. He was getting tired of talking. Tired of speculation. Ready to move on. "So what?"

"Nothing. I don't know why I even mentioned it." He pointed down the dark hallway. "Listen, we should start knocking doors."

*

Franco took the first floor and drew the unlucky card of interviewing Mrs. Donato, in Apartment 1A. And her cats, all 17 of them.

"Yes?" She stood in the doorway, ancient in smudged glasses, a floral-print housecoat, and slippers. Behind her, the living room teamed with felines.

"Mrs. Donato?"

"I would open the door wider," she said, "but I'm afraid Bambino and Misty will make a run for it. Last time they got out, it was three days before I saw them again."

"Let's not let that happen, then. I'm Detective Lopinto. May I come in?"

She unlocked the deadbolt and the door just wide enough for Franco to slide in, sideways. He winced at the smell of Este Lauder perfume mixed with kitty litter. It was fucking horrible, but he tried not to let it show. "Mrs. Donato, do you know many of your neighbors?"

"I do. I've been here nine years, since Mr. Donato

passed." She shielded her mouth with one hand and whispered, "Colon cancer." She reached down and grabbed Bambino, a large orange and white cat with a ringed tail. Bambino squirmed in her arms, but she held him tightly. "Would you like some tea and biscotti, Officer?"

Franco shook his head and flipped open his notepad. He lowered himself onto a fur-coated Victorian-looking settee. "Mrs. Donato—"

"There weren't many synthetic people living here back then. It wasn't even called Doherty Boulevard, and certainly not the Dirty Boulevard. It was Columbus Parkway. Did you know that?"

"Let's get back to your neighbors, Mrs. Donato. Do you know Rachel Montgomery? In apartment 2C."

"Oh, Rachel. A beautiful girl."

"Did she have a boyfriend or a partner of some kind?"

"Lots of boyfriends." She pursed her lips to show how scandalous it was for a young woman to have lots of boyfriends.

"Any that you remember in particular? Maybe one who came to visit her last night, or this morning?" A tortoise shell cat climbed onto his lap. He pushed it away, but it jumped right back.

She shook her head. "Do you know what, Detective?"

Franco sighed. Mrs. Donato was about to go off the rails. Worse, Bambino had hissed the tortoise shell cat away and taken her place. He was purring, and kneading his claws into Franco's pants. Eighteen filthy little needles going in and out. "What's that, Mrs. Donato?"

"If I were her age, I would have as many boyfriends, too. I used to be quite beautiful, you know."

Jesus, in what freaking century? Franco tapped his pen on the notebook. "Did Rachel have any kind of trouble with these boyfriends, Mrs. Donato? Or anyone else for that matter? You know, fights or arguments in the hallway? Maybe shouting from inside the apartment? Things like that."

"No, nothing that I can remember." She covered her cheeks with her hands. "She's dead, isn't she? I saw the police lights."

Franco rose and brushed the cat off his lap. He stood before the window and pulled back the shades, expecting the panes to be covered with dust. They were clean. "Do you open the blinds often, Mrs. Donato?"

She kept her hands on her cheeks. "Oh, yes. The cats like to watch for birds, you know, but they also watch people." The window was nailed shut, but it gave a view of the sidewalk, as well as the parking spaces on both side of the Boulevard.

Franco closed the drapes and returned to the settee. Bambino eyed him suspiciously. Something was a little off about the beast, but he couldn't tell what. "On second thought, Ms. Donato, I will have some tea and biscotti. And you can tell me all about your cats. I'm especially interested in what he looks at outside that window."

A Forever Opposition

Sean Connell

I decided that I was gonna kill the guy about nine months ago. I assumed the murder would be retold in the news as a husband's revenge, and that was the truth, but I was worried I'd be portrayed as a pathetic cuckhold, which was not the truth. This was vengeance, and I'd made my peace with that, and whatever my consequences were to be, in this world and wherever else too.

The Halloween party was the first big social event I'd attended since my wife, Bethany, died. My buddy Mike and his wife, Lidia, had recently renovated a Federalist style home on High Street in Newburyport. I figured most guests, like me, understood Lidia's true motivation for the party was to show off her new statement house while triumphantly announcing her return to her hometown.

"I'm so happy to see you," Mike said, holding me in an extended, genuine embrace. "I didn't believe Lidia when she said you'd RSVP'd. I made her show me the Facebook confirmation."

*

After Bethany died, the airline told me, "Take as much time as you need, Captain." I took their offer literally and discovered the arrangement was finite. In my first weeks as an unemployed, childless widower, I wallowed in double cheeseburgers from Wendy's and nightly magnums of

Woodbridge Cab. I wanted to list our condo at a price to sell and just get the hell out of there, but, after eighteen months, I still hadn't left.

Bethany was one of six kids, so my in-laws quickly faded from my life. That wasn't so bad. My parents and siblings tried to intervene during my months of isolation, but I forced them away, sometimes with hostility. If I was going to be punished after death, this is what I figured it would be for.

The longer I didn't see anyone besides the Wendy's drive-thru lady and the fat liquor store guy, the more my last memories before Bethany's overdose sharpened.

"I'm sorry for what I did to you," Bethany said and sobbed, rolling around on our bed, too high to make sense.

"What'd you do?"

"Trev," Bethany said, "listen, listen. Forgive me."

"Forgive you for what?"

"Nobody deserves that."

"Nobody deserves what?"

"Say you forgive me," Bethany said. "I need it. I need to hear it."

The Oxy was no secret anymore. After her first trip to rehab, some even learned about the heroin. Remembering her withdrawals and thinking about the poor nurses who'd have to clean up were all I could think about when I dropped her off at the hospital. I will remember forever the smell of that particular vomit, while holding back all her thick, curly brown hair. After the puking she'd start an endless loop of stoned apologizing until she passed out. A few glasses of wine and a movie helped me fall asleep on the sofa on those nights. But sometimes I couldn't cope with not knowing what she felt so terrible about, and I'd go into the bedroom and scream at Bethany to tell me what she was so sorry for, or to just shut the fuck up so I could sleep.

*

Mike, costumed as Shrek, looked phenomenal. Lidia was down the hallway, dressed as Princess Fiona. When she saw me in the foyer, she excused herself from her conversation and rushed to give me a big, fake hug.

"We're just so thrilled you came," Lidia said. "The guest room on the third floor is all made up for you. No one else even knows it's available."

"You do have a talent for making sleeping arrangements," I said, hoping one last time she was brighter than I thought.

Lidia tilted her head and smiled, looking a bit stunned. "Mike," she said, "be helpful. Get Trevor a drink."

Mike put his arm around me and guided us into the parlor. "What're you drinking these days?"

"A seltzer water would be great," I said. "But on ice, please, and in a rocks glass? Our secret?"

*

Sometime soon after Bethany's funeral, in the blur of a Tuesday night Woodbridge-magnum-self-challenge, I got preoccupied with the timeline. Bethany was in a head-on car accident about a year-and-a-half ago, in February. Her doctor called her lucky because she somehow only broke her ankle, although she broke-the-living-shit out of her ankle. After her surgery, she was referred to a Podiatrist named Daniel Gannon, whom I never met but never fucking liked either. Dr. Danny prescribed OxyContin for the post-operation pain. Bethany, fearful of addiction, told me that she mentioned her alcoholic uncle to Dr. Danny, but he said he'd only prescribed ten days of pills, and that wasn't enough to create an ongoing dependence. But Bethany had pills until her first trip to rehab in May.

*

Mike handed me a soda water on the rocks, clapping me on the back. "You've been lifting," Mike said, squeezing my shoulders.

"Running, too," I said. "I've found new purpose. But I rolled my ankle last month, and it's been slowing me down. Haven't yet had a chance to get it looked at."

Mike sipped his beer, "I'll introduce you to Danny Gannon. He's one of the doctors that Lidia works with at the hospital. He's actually from Salisbury, but he was ahead of us in school. He hooks me up, mostly Viagra. I call him Dr. Feel Good."

*

Bethany's phone gave up all the crushing details that I didn't need. Unsurprisingly, it was Lidia who kicked the first pebble of the rockslide. After Bethany's first appointment with Dr. Danny, Lidia texted her, "He just asked me if ur married!! Hunk! Right?"

One of the first texts from Bethany's contact "DFG" was in late March. It read, "Physical therapy today?"

"Yes!!" Bethany wrote back. "Where can we exercise? ;)"

The weekly text exchanges with DFG continued into May.

"In the mood for some HOT yoga?" DFG wrote.

"You're so bad. Your office? Can you write me a script?"

*

The floors in Lidia's parlor were refinished vintage parquet that reflected the dim yellow overhead bulbs. In one corner of the room there was the full-sized statue of a sentry knight's armor. In the other corner, a built-in bar connected to the wainscoting of the same deep brown finish. Despite the overpowering smell of lemon Pledge, the detailed woodwork that stretched around the room made me feel like I was somewhere exclusive, somewhere secret.

"You're from Salisbury?" Dr. Danny Gannon finally asked me. "The *wrong* side of the river."

"True."

"Did you go to Triton High?"

"I did."

Dr. Danny was well over six-feet tall, lean like a competitive cyclist, and was more handsome in person than his pictures, which was a brutal additional detail. He was twelve years older than me, but he looked more youthful. He had sharp features and a frequent dimpled smile, checking all the boxes that turned Bethany on.

"That's perfect then," Dr. Danny said, finishing his beer, "that means we both have world class educations."

"Can I get you another drink?" Mike asked from behind the bar.

"You know, that's a great costume," Dr. Danny said. "I didn't like the movie, but *Fear and Loathing* is one of my all-time favorite books."

I knew that *Fear and Loathing* in Las Vegas was one of

Dr. Danny's favorite books because I'd been following him for fifty-three weeks and four days. I also knew The Sopranos was his favorite TV show, that he surprisingly hated the Marvel Universe movies although he loved films about time travel, and that he didn't like to fly but he was an excellent swimmer, so drowning him was out of the question.

"It's my long-running, short notice go-to costume," I said. "All you need are khaki shorts, a Hawaiian shirt, and the green visor."

Mike held out a Manhattan, and when Danny reached for the drink his costume's coat-sleeve pulled back from his wrist and revealed a shirt cuff embroidered with the initials, *DFG*.

Now anyone could assume that Daniel Gannon's middle name would be Francis. I did. But it's actually Fournier, which was his mother's maiden name as well as the name of his favorite dog when he was a kid. And not only were DFG his initials by birth, but they were also the inspiration for his nickname with nurses and ex-lovers, which was a reference to both his practices in medicine and personal matters. To all those that he chose to work with, Daniel Fournier Gannon was Dr. Feel Good. He was DFG in name and image.

"But, then again," Danny said, and sipped his drink, "I suppose any Halloween costume is better than a doctor dressed as a doctor."

"I wouldn't worry about it," I said. "The costumes have nothing to do with why we're all here," and I gave Mike an apology wink.

"Is that right?" Danny said, smiling at Mike. "You mean to tell me that this whole thing wasn't his call?"

"The house, the party, or both?" I asked.

"Call it the whole fucking thing," Danny said, and he

pulled his wavy blond hair from his forehead. "But, to be fair, let's review Mike's situation. Option 1, he can cash out his life's savings and move to his wife's hometown, which he hates, or –"

"He could've cashed out his life's savings via divorce," Mike said, his elbow on the bar, his chin in his palm.

"You look like *I* need a drink," Danny said, and then he turned to me. "So, Mike says you're dealing with a busted ankle?"

*

"Ankle isn't better. Need you to WORK me out ;)" Bethany had texted.

"Shit. Not sure if I can today. Tomm?" DFG replied.

"Quick PT session? For me??" And Bethany sent a playful nude.

"Oh wow. Okay. I'll cancel my appt before lunch. My place."

"Script too?"

"DFG is in."

*

Danny's house was a little cape, built in the twenties and on the riverside of his street. He bought it with perfect timing, precisely at the bottom of the market. He renovated it from the outside first, then the inside. After my first few stakeouts, I realized that if Danny was home, the basement lights were on. So that quickly became my biggest curiosity.

When I broke into Danny's house for the first time, I didn't learn much because the basement door was locked and the rest of the house looked unoccupied. The main floor and the upstairs were always spotless. Not a single dust bunny in a corner, the glass everywhere was always smudgeless, everything always in its right place, and the inside stairs never creaked, not even once on any of my visits (and by my last time inside I was really trying to find a squeaker). The place was either staged for an open house or a fucking trap. But, when I finally found the key to the basement, I understood the upstairs.

The basement was entirely unfinished, a hard, rocky space that smelled like the riverbank and felt like being dripped on. Despite that, one side was furnished to be lived in, arranged as a combination bedroom and living room. He had a TV and an Xbox down there and the remotes were always evenly placed on the right corner of his coffee table. Inside the drawer of the coffee table, he hid a small green journal where he'd written the names of women, some with a specific date next them. He wrote one name per line, double spaced, and had a few pages worth. The last entry read:

*Bethany O'Ryan, divorced*_____

On the other side of the basement, well on the other side of the basement, there was this lamplit habitat with tanks and tanks and tanks of spiders, scorpions, centipedes, crabs, and all sorts of other hideous looking shit with too many legs and too many eyes. One wall was covered in dead butterflies under wax paper. Another wall was covered with dozens of horseshoe crab shells. But, somehow, this space got inside of me. When I was away from it, I felt the tug of an addiction. All those visits and all that time I spent sitting on the floor in there, surrounded by all that instinctual life comforted me in accepting what my nature was telling me to do. All those creatures, incapable of judgement beyond nature was what I needed to finally abandon the burdensome empathy that had been holding me back.

*

"You know," Danny said, "when I first met Lidia, she said to me something like, *You're from Salisbury? How come you don't have an accent like they do?* Like we speak a different language."

"Like you're a different species."

"She is hot though," Danny said. "Wouldn't you love to fuck her? Especially in that costume?"

We'd withdrawn to a small reading room with built-in bookshelves and a lone, oval stained-glass window. The blue, green, yellow, and red panels pictured a frog carrying a scorpion across a pond.

"You married?" Danny asked.

"Nope."

"Divorced?"

"Nope."

"Feels like you're still bouncing back from one," Danny said. "I kinda get that."

He was standing at the colorful, pendant shaped window, studying it. "They get a bad rap," he said. "Most people don't know that mother scorpions carry offspring on their backs until their exoskeletons harden."

"Feels like a lot of compassion for a scorpion."

"Exactly my point," Danny said. "It's surprising to hear that scorpions care for their babies until they're ready for the world because that's like you, right? But in their case, it's not compassion. It's just their nature. Yet, the frog won't understand because they both drown."

Danny walked over and handed me one of the Manhattans he was holding.

"Thanks, but I'm a clear-spirits only guy."

"Fuck that," Danny said. "Drink that. Get wrecked with me."

I took the martini glass to my mouth. "Hm," I said when I sipped the trembling liquid away from the rim, "that first taste always has a sting."

"The sting won't kill you," Danny said, "but the pinchers will," and he snapped his fingers like claws, backlit by the colorful panels of the window. He dropped himself into a scarlet corduroy chair with brass buttons. "This fucking party is gonna kill me, and I'm gonna be too bombed to fake a good time after this one."

"Let's disappear then," I said. "Let's go to the strippy."

Danny gently bobbed his head as he thought it over. "Just a couple of Salisbury kids going to the strip club."

"Everything in its right place," I said.

"Tens or Kittens?"

"Your call."

Danny leaned back into the worn back of the corduroy. "I feel like slumming it."

I tucked my costume's green visor and aviator sunglasses into the center console. Danny sat in the passenger seat, vacantly looking out the window at the passing streetlights as we drove north on Route 1 towards Kittens. Danny was drunk, but he was working hard at trying not to be totally shitfaced.

"You sure you're okay to drive?" Danny asked. "You drank almost as much as me, and I definitely am not driving.

But, I would've paid for the ride, or whatever."

I took Bridge Road over the Merrimack River. A steady line of traffic driving south passed us along the unlit, undivided state highway.

"They're not gonna know what to make of us," Danny laughed, "a couple of costumed assholes."

"You mentioned a breakup at the party," I said. "What happened?"

"What didn't," Danny said. "I could've lost my medical license." Danny rubbed his hands over his face. "A while back now, I was sleeping with this woman –"

"Like a steady girlfriend?"

"Uh, no," Danny said. "Honestly, I only sleep with married chicks. I get off on being a homewrecker. It's fucked up, I know. Anyways, I was sleeping with this woman who'd been in a car accident that just fucking destroyed her ankle, and then the hack surgeon made it worse. I wrote her a few additional prescriptions for the pain, but then she couldn't get off the pills. I wanted to help, but, dude, when she was high, she got fucking wild in the sack."

From the other side of the highway, pairs of yellow-golden headlights zipped past us like photons. Danny's eyes were sagging and glassy as he tried to focus on the road ahead, the oncoming headlights illuminating his face, then leaving it in darkness.

"Did she overdose?"

"Oh, yeah," Danny said. "Like, fast. Like, five months from the first prescription."

"Did you kill her?"

Danny scoffed. "She fucking killed herself."

That's when I gave up on my plan and I let the car drift over the yellow line, into the southbound lane. The first

87

oncoming car missed us by swerving onto the northbound side. That was fine because it was a coupe, and it wasn't guaranteed to kill us. But the second vehicle was a big truck with a big grill, its headlights closing in on us, its horn in a constant roar, and then Danny yanked the steering wheel to the right and I lost control of the car, spinning across the northbound lane, over the shoulder of the highway, through a chain link fence, and coming to a convenient stop in the parking lot of Kittens Gentlemen's Club.

*

Danny was sitting next to me on the ground in Kittens' parking lot. The flashing blue and red lights were disorienting.

"Zero, point zero," the state trooper said into the receiver clipped to his left breast. "The other one's gassed, but he wasn't driving."

Behind the officer, two half-dressed dancers, shivering beneath furry overcoats, were talking to a detective. "I seen it," one of the dancers said. "I seen the whole thing. The white boy in the Hawaiian shirt drove into the other lane. Then that big ass truck swerved outta the road and into the building."

About a quarter mile to my left, a super-duty pickup truck had driven through the front wall of a dry cleaners. To my right, in the flashing strobes of siren lights, a rugged, bearded, and bald black man in a white suit and a gold tie walked across the parking lot. He nodded at both detectives before standing over me and Danny, helping us to our feet.

"I'm thinking neither of you would object to some individual attention, a special interaction," he said. "My name is Mr. Pedro, and this is my place." Mr. Pedro removed a pen and a white spiral steno pad from his suitcoat. "I don't want there to be confusion about who's receiving my considerations, so, traveler number one, what's your name?"

"Trevor."

"I see you, Trevor O.," Mr. Pedro said, drawing three stars and a question mark next to my name. Then he looked at Danny. "And just what the hell are you?" he asked.

"It was a costume party," Danny said.

"That sure ain't what I was asking," Mr. Pedro said, replacing his white notebook. He removed another small, spiral ringed booklet with a black cover, took a moment and looked into Danny. Then he drew a calligraphed "M," accented with a triangle-tipped tail curling up from the right stem of the letter. "But I see you now. I see both you now."

Glowing in the distance above the red velvet entry rope, "KITTENS GENTLEMEN'S CLUB Cold Girls, Hot Beer, Loitering Encouraged" was illuminated on the side of the concrete building with bright, white neon tubes. Mr. Pedro shook the bouncer's hand and guided Danny down the stairwell that sank towards the underground entrance.

The bouncer stopped me and patted down the sides of my torso, squeezing all my pockets. "Twenty-dollar cover."

"Nah, not for him," Mr. Pedro yelled from down the stairwell. "That one's with me, too."

The bouncer looked me over, from eyelids to toes. "Nice outfit, honkey. What're you supposed to be?"

"On a self-righteous downward spiral, but this isn't exactly Vegas."

"Yo, seriously," Mr. Pedro yelled at the bouncer, "he'll kill your ass, for real."

At the bottom of the stairs, the wall perpendicular to the

door was painted to be a chalkboard with "Twelve Pearl Vodka! $1 SHOT SPECIAL!" written in red and bright pink. The door to get inside looked like the entry to a padded room. It was iron bracketed by iron, with a speakeasy grille that shrieked upwards, and then snapped down like a guillotine just before the door was unlocked.

The club was full and the song that vibrated through the steaming underworld told us to have a cigar. Bodies parted for Mr. Pedro as he led me and Danny through the crowd. The floor was bowed and covered in glossy black tile. A shade of unwashed red darkened the walls that were decorated with framed portraits. A wide-eyed Kalashnikov hung next to a shot-up Jimi Hendrix. Not far away was a stoned-looking Einstein buried in work alongside his student, Oppenheimer.

"And you got Quincy Adams, Nobel, Hermann Mueller, Alex The Great, all autographed, all authentic," Mr. Pedro said. "My most famous guests, and it ain't like they just popped in and popped out. They *needed* Mr. Pedro."

A checkered path of red squares weaved around the black load-bearing poles, each one decorated with bizarre stick figures that appeared to wrinkle and ripple on their own.

"These are my personal seats," Mr. Pedro said, pulling out two front row chairs.

The classic rock song faded away and the dancer scrambled along the stage to collect they sprays of cash. The DJ encouraged the crowd to get extra excited for Kittens' headliner for the night, who appeared behind a cheap mist, wearing a smart pantsuit and exaggerated eyeglasses.

Mr. Pedro slapped Danny on the shoulder, but Danny was asleep. He then turned to me. "Yo," he said, "you know who you're with?"

A waitress interrupted, asking Mr. Pedro for his drink order. Her hair was artificial blond, worn up in a bun, most likely a wig. She was short, nimble, her features hidden beneath layers of concealing makeup.

"Two Jim and gingers, please," Mr. Pedro said.

"Actually, I'm a clear-spirits only guy –"

"That's a joke," Mr. Pedro said to the waitress.

Kittens' headliner had just thrown away her academic blouse, and she'd latched herself onto the front pole, spinning downward as her eighties ballad hit its chorus.

"Do you know who this is?" Mr. Pedro asked, motioning to Danny.

"Yeah."

"And?"

"He's a local doctor," I said. "We met at a party."

"Shit," Mr. Pedro said. "You don't know where you are."

"I'm a little stunned, sure," I said. "You offered a dance. I didn't think to say no, and –"

"It's all good, homie. We'll let it breathe for a beat."

With two plastic cups overflowing with ginger ale and Jim Beam, the waitress leaned into our station, placing two cocktail napkins on the table between us and setting down our drinks.

"Do you two know each other?" Mr. Pedro asked.

"How could we?" I said.

"Small world shit," Mr. Pedro said. "Baby girl, do you know my man?"

The waitress looked away, towards the ceiling of exposed beams and pipes, bedecked with dusty spiderwebs that were pushed and pulled by the ceiling fans that distributed the mixed stink of body odor and hair spray.

"Baby girl," Mr. Pedro said, "I need your help."

The waitress glanced back and shook her head.

"That's all right," Mr. Pedro said, "everything's got its price in this place."

The party-era power chords faded, and Mr. Pedro took me by the elbow and turned me towards the waitress. "Baby Girl," Mr. Pedro said, "I need your help reorientating my guest."

The waitresses' shoulders rose and fell as she gathered herself. She raised her left hand towards her forehead and pulled away her wig, letting her long, thick brown curls fall beyond her shoulders.

I smelled her vomit in our old bathroom when I saw that hair.

"Hey, Trev," Bethany said. "You're here sooner than expected."

I pushed my way out of the chair and dodged through the crowd, maneuvering between bodies, beams, tables, and chairs. I bounded up the concrete stairs to the street level and saw that the accident scene had changed. A super-duty truck with a smashed frontend straddled the yellow dividing line. A few feet away was my car, only half as long as it once was. Police took pictures and placed markers on the ground while a trio of medics arranged three full body bags next to each other in the road.

Ahead of us, on the horizon, an orange star was rising, buzzing and determined, just beginning its escape from the twilight's last rays, unwilling to be stopped before reaching the night sky. Over my shoulder, the up-tempo clicking of Bethany's high heels approached, accompanied by Mr. Pedro. Bethany was composed, and focused on Mr. Pedro.

"What's the world's oldest job?" Mr. Pedro asked.

"Prostitution," I said.

"Wrong," Mr. Pedro said. "It's gatekeeping. Beginning with the Assyrians, Sumerians, Babylonians—the motherfucking Mesopotamians—ancient Egyptians, Greeks, Romans, Jews, Vikings, Celts, Muslims, and Christians all understood that a fare was to be paid to some sentry somewhere in exchange for traveling the dimensions back to the physical world. I told you this is my place, and therefore I am your sentry."

Mr. Pedro rolled his shoulders as he adjusted his tie.

"So, I pay you money?"

"Homie, do you understand metaphor?"

"A fare can be a sacrifice or a settlement," Bethany said.

"But it's gotta be the right one," Mr. Pedro said.

Bethany was done-up like a cartoon. Stiletto heels, glitter in her makeup, and a cocktail dress that was barely lower than her crotch. In our other life, if she saw another woman dressed like this, she would've said, "Girl, it's not your fault no one taught you to respect yourself." What a fall from grace for Bethany. What a hypocrite she became while rolling around on our bed and apologizing to me.

"I think I know what to do," I said.

"All right, homeboy," Mr. Pedro said, "work the puzzle."

"Bethany," I said, "I forgive you."

I looked at Mr. Pedro. He looked at Bethany, and Bethany looked at him.

"Was that for you?" Mr. Pedro asked. "Or was that for her?"

"That was for her."

"For me?" Bethany said. "I don't need you to forgive me. Do you know why I married you? A misguided desire for stature. I thought a young, woman executive married to a young, handsome, veteran pilot was the life I was entitled to. But then I realized you were incapable of making anyone but yourself feel loved. So, yeah, I had an affair, and it was fucking hot. What I regret is my guilt in the first place, and that I thought I needed you to accept it."

"Damn," Mr. Pedro said, letting the word drift around us.

Bethany looked down at herself as she slowly began to disappear. She turned to Mr. Pedro, her mouth moving in a silent "Thank you." And then she was gone.

"I was really trying to help," I said.

"You did help," Mr. Pedro said, "just not the way you intended."

"Am I stuck here now?" I asked. "In Hell, with you?"

"Stuck, for now," Mr. Pedro said. "But there ain't really Hell. Or, think of Hell as a matter of perspective. Some souls will never experience Hell. Others will only ever be in Hell. By the sounds of your previous marriage, maybe you've already been through Hell, and this place is just a rickety bridge back to life."

"But I can't do it on my own."

"Settling the past life often takes at least one partner," Mr. Pedro said.

The rising star in front of us had deepened its unique color to a scorched russet, like leaves in a gutter, distinguishing it from the others in the sky, and making it obvious that appearance was not a part of its mission.

"What the fuck is this?" Danny had just jogged up to us. We looked over the body bags together. His face was moist and colorless.

"Did you see a dead girl in there?" I asked.

"Are you a part of this?"

"We're all a part of this," Mr. Pedro said. "Danny, what's

the oldest job in the world?"

Danny's chest rose and fell. After a moment of thought, he huffed his surrender.

"Most souls say, prostitution."

Danny looked beyond Mr. Pedro, distracted when the loudness of the sky was interrupted by a passing cloud that dimmed the rising star's color from a bold, humming persimmon to a gritty auburn.

"Fuck this," Danny said, and he brushed past Mr. Pedro. He walked southbound with confidence, looking steady, sober, and strengthening.

Nonetheless, I was still going to kill him. Even the idea of being banished to mop the floors at Kittens for eternity wasn't enough to deter me. To finally kill Dr. Danny Gannon felt correct, inevitable, an act with a higher purpose, and I couldn't make myself care about settling that future debt on my soul.

"Yo, Danny," Mr. Pedro yelled.

Danny's middle finger replied.

"You're not in control here, homie."

"Then why do I feel so fucking powerful?" Danny yelled back.

"Powerful?" Mr. Pedro said, looking to the rising star as it culminated along its path, tired and rusted from its offensive, but undoubtedly established in its position. "Danny! There's a difference between gatekeeping and soul catching. If you don't listen, my job becomes the latter."
Mr. Pedro's gaze followed Danny past the last remnants of the accident scene, far enough away to be almost completely hidden by the blackness in between the streetlights.

"All right," Mr. Pedro said to me, "you wanna witness some wild shit? Follow Danny's shadow. Watch when it comes under the white light."

Danny dropped to a knee when he entered the conical beam of the next streetlight. He began to shake, like an animal about to burst. His arms wrapped around his stomach, and he rocked back and forth with a subtle orbit, around and around, before clumsily scuttling forward, almost out of sight.

"Don't look away," Mr. Pedro said, "here comes your partner."

Danny's progress was more heard than seen, the sounds of shuffling and crawling as Danny tripped forward across the dirt of the highway's shoulder until he was gone. The air went silent for a moment, but there came a slow and deliberate patter, like aggravated fingertips on a desk. Unsteady ticking noises followed, tapping like ski poles along the asphalt. Mr. Pedro moved away, pressing me backwards along with him. From the unlit side of the highway and into the streetlight crept the rounded edge of a giant pincer claw, followed by the silhouette of an enormous scorpion that inched itself into the halo of the streetlight. The scorpion angled its body northward and moved forward through the light, sending a flash of turquoise fluorescence across its black exoskeleton. It raised its tail over its mesosoma, and then waited flawlessly still.

"I'll be damned if I know how that thing keeps getting back into bodies," Mr. Pedro said. "You too, I'm sure."

"What is it?"

"That's your boy," Mr. Pedro said. "That's Danny, the yang to your ying. The thing you gotta resolve unless it resolves you first."

"How?"

"Who knows," Mr. Pedro said. "This ongoing stalemate

of y'all's almost at the two millennia mark."

The scorpion sank down into its striking pose, waiting for movement, feeling for vibration. The streetlight illuminated its mouth parts and eye group, and the scorpion's left legs twitched in sequence before it sidled away from the highway and into the darkness.

"All right, homie." Mr. Pedro said. "Start from the beginning. How'd the two of you get here this time?"

The star overhead had reached full redness. Spherical like an antique bullet, its perimeter metallic, droning, and radiating a heat that vibrated against my chest.

"I decided that I was gonna kill the guy about nine months ago."

Biographies

Celeste White is a freelance writer and editor, artist, and art director for a community health center. She is the author of *The Legend of the Flying Hotdog*, selected by Parents magazine as one of the Best Kids' Books of the year, and *The Last Good Fairy*, a multi-media project that involved a fine collectible edition of a novel and a treasure hunt for four pieces of found-object art hidden in different parts of the US. The novel was awarded a New England Book Show Award for excellence in book design. She is also the co-founder and publisher of a small literary journal, *The Hot Air Quarterly* that was in circulation from 2006 – 2011. She lives in northern California.

Louise Kantro, a retired high school English teacher, is a bridge-player, cat-lover, and CASA (Court Appointed Special Advocate for foster children). She received her MFA from Goddard College in 2003, and has published poetry and prose in such journals and anthologies as *Quercus Review*, *Cloudbank*, *Oasis*, *The Chariton Review*, *the new renaissance*, *South Loop Review*, and *Caesura*.

Outside of her day job as a phlebotomist, **Kathryn (Katie) Tomasko** fervently works at writing novels, poetry, and fine arts. A graduate of Southern New Hampshire University with a Bachelor's in game design, she has completed a novel-length poetry book, illustrated by her own drawings. A genre-jumper at heart, she has two more projects—a massive fantasy-adventure book and a literary fiction novella—that are nearing completion. When not writing, she obeys the whims of her Great Dane Ellie and consumes inspirational media, be it art, shows, books, or life. Whatever she does during the day to pay the bills, writing will always be her passion and greatest love. You can find her on Instagram at katie.t.author to follow along with her writing and art journeys.

Shawn Goodman is the author of *Kindness for Weakness*, *Something Like Hope*, which won the '09 Delacorte Prize, and *This Way Home*, written with Wes Moore, also by Delacorte. His short fiction has appeared in *The Bitter Oleander*, *Bayou*, and *JMWW*. He lives in Ithaca, NY, with his family.

Sean Connell has published previously in *The Bangalore Review* and *Bird's Thumb*. He received his BA in English from Clark University and his MFA in fiction from Southern New Hampshire University.

Contest Finalists

Author	Manuscript Title
Esinam Bediako	Vera, Your Man Is History
Cynthia Young	A Mother's Guide to Dying
Dev Jannerson	Charity Starts at Home
Marc Olivere	Sidekick
David Norling	Ghost Karamazov
Carolyn Dasher	American Girls
Greg Bayer	Return to Baghdad
Frank DiPalermo	Singing in Tongues
Adina Baker	The Button Thief
Christine Wade	Charm of Finches
Chuck Boyer	The Islands of Not Having
Richard Fellinger	An American Girl
Kim Merrill	Where Is Marie?
Kent Kosack	Contour, Gesture, Line

Congratulations to the winners and finalists, and our deepest appreciation for all who entered—the decision-making process was extremely difficult at every stage.

Supporters

Novel Slices would like to thank our generous supporters, without whom this issue would not have been possible.

Burcu Gurkan
Christiaan F. Batten
Alex Snell
Jonathan Berzer
Nermin Mollaoğlu
Remy J. Alan
Ahmet Yıldız
Susanna Drbal
Jeanne Mackin
Haluk Şengeç
Nancy Holzner
Eric Darton
Bill Hayword
Bekir Erol Ateş
Burcu Ünsal
Christophe Hille
Banu Özer Griffin

Interested in advertising in *Novel Slices*? Reach out to us to discuss: novelslices@gmail.com.

CPSIA information can be obtained
at www.ICGtesting.com
Printed in the USA
LVHW041024070223
738747LV00002B/7

9 781088 089385